MEET THE GIRL TALK CHARACTERS

Sabrina Wells is petite, with curly auburn hair, sparkling hazel eyes, and a bubbly personality. Sabrina loves magazines, shopping, sleepovers, and most of all, she loves talking to her best friends.

Katie Campbell is a straight-A student and super athlete. With her blond hair, blue eyes, and matching clothes, she's everyone's idea of Little Miss Perfect. But Katie has a few surprises for everyone, including herself!

Randy Zak has just moved to Acorn Falls from New York City, and is she ever cool! With her radical spiked haircut and her hip New York clothes, Randy teaches everyone just how much fun it is to be different.

Allison Cloud is a Native American Indian. Allison's supersmart and really beautiful. But she has one major problem: She's thirteen years old, five foot seven, and still growing!

COUSINS

By L. E. Blair

GIRL TALK® series created by Western Publishing Company, Inc.

Western Publishing Company, Inc., Racine, Wisconsin 53404

R MCMXCIII

Text by Carol McCarren

Chapter One

"Hey, Sabs! Are you ever coming out of there?" my twin brother, Sam, shouted through the bathroom door.

I turned my blow dryer up to the highest speed. "I can't hear you!" I called.

"Then how do you know I'm talking to you?" Sam yelled back. He was pounding on the door so hard, I thought it was going to fall off its hinges.

It was a typical Saturday morning in the Wells household. There I was in the bathroom, struggling to subdue the curly red mop I call my hair. Every Saturday I start extra early, hoping to get a little more time. And every Saturday Sam seems to get the exact same idea.

I mean, I know we're twins — we have the same red hair and freckles — but do we always have to have the same brilliant ideas?

Actually, I had to rush despite Sam pounding on the door. I was meeting my best friends, Katie, Randy, and Allison, at the mall, like I always do on Saturdays. And, as usual, I was running late! But I couldn't wait to tell them the big news about my chic cousin from France, who was coming to visit for a few weeks. I was so excited! This was one time I didn't want to be late. And I needed Sam rushing me like I needed an attack of the frizzies. Which was what I was going to get if he didn't let me finish drying my hair!

"Face it, Sabs, the only thing your hair is good for is hatching baby birds!" Sam shouted. "Give it up already!"

"Okay! Okay!" I sighed. I turned off the dryer and yanked the door open. My yellow-and-black sweater was on the towel rack. I started pulling it on over my T-shirt. "Honestly, Sam! A girl can't get any peace around this house," I muttered.

"Hey, Sabs, Katie called and said that you and Allison should meet her and Randy in front of the pizza shop," Sam informed me. Then he grabbed my two empty sweater sleeves and tied them in a knot over my head.

"Cut it out, Sam!" I yelled. "I can't see!" I

waved my arms around and tried to pull the rest of the sweater down past my eyes.

"Just walk straight," said Sam. He grabbed my shoulders and directed me out of the bathroom.

"C'mon, Sam! Untie my sweater! You're going to make me late!" I pleaded, bumping into the wall.

"Oh! And I forgot to tell you," he called after me, "Katie said to make sure you don't wear that horrible yellow-and-black-striped thing that makes you look like an overgrown bumblebee." With that Sam slammed the bathroom door shut behind him.

"Yeah! Right!" I mumbled under my breath. I knew Sam was just teasing, and I didn't really mind. When you have four brothers, you get used to being teased. As my mom always says, "That's just their way of showing affection."

I finally managed to work my arms into the sleeves and pull the rest of the sweater down over my head. Then I checked out the effect in the hallway mirror. I really liked my "bumblebee" sweater. And it looked especially cool with my black leggings. It was a perfect "Saturday-at-the-Mall" outfit.

I ran my hand through my hair. It was still a little damp. My hair is auburn, and really thick and curly, so it takes forever to dry. I grabbed a towel and tried to smooth it down. But it just kept getting fluffier and fluffier. Hello, frizzies!

Just as I was trying to decide if I should wet it and blow-dry it all over again, the doorbell rang. I knew it had to be my friend Allison Cloud. Her dad was giving us a ride to the mall. I grabbed my bag and ran down to meet her.

"Cool outfit," Allison commented as soon as she saw me.

"Thanks, Al. Love your boots," I said. She was wearing these great brown-and-gold cowboy boots. They looked really awesome with her tan fringed jacket, stone-washed jeans, and long black braid. I think boots look great when you're tall like Allison. She's almost a foot taller than me! I'm almost five feet tall, and I tried on a pair of Al's over-the-knee boots once. They made me look like I was walking on stilts!

We drove over to the mall and headed toward the pizza shop. I saw Katie right away. As usual, she was on time and waiting for all of us. She was wearing a really cool red-and-green-plaid jumper. It had these great shoulder straps that went up over a baggy white blouse. She had a red-and-green headband in her gorgeous honey-blond hair and even red-and-green tights! Katie is always so coordinated, I just don't know how she does it!

"And heeere's Randy," called my other best friend Randy Zak as she rounded the corner on her skateboard. She came to an abrupt halt right in front of us. That's when I got a really good look at her.

"Wow! That's radical!" I exclaimed. Randy had shocks of purple running through her spiky black hair. She was wearing a huge purple sweater over her usual black leggings. Dangling from her ears were awesome earrings. They looked like strips of film that had been cut from a black-and-white movie. Randy always has to have something in her outfit that's black. It's probably because she's from New York City. Everyone's cool there, and I guess they wear a lot of black.

"How did you do that?" Allison wondered. She gingerly patted the top of Randy's head.

"It's just a spray," Randy stated. "My friend Sheck sent me a bunch of different colors." Then she saw Allison's face. "Don't fret yourself, Al, it'll wash out by tomorrow. And then maybe I'll try orange, or yellow, or blue. . . . "

"I think it's cool," said Katie. "But I don't think my mom would go for it." Katie's mom just remarried, so Katie's whole life has sort of changed. She still lives in Acorn Falls, but now she lives in a big mansion with servants and everything. Not exactly the place for purple hair.

"So what's the big news?" Katie asked as we squeezed into a bright blue booth at Pauley's Pizza Parlor.

"Yeah," Allison cut in. "You said this was really a big one."

"It is," I said. "Remember when I told you I had a cousin who lives in Paris?"

"You mean the one that's the model?" asked Allison.

"Right, that one," I replied.

"And she has this really weird name, like Zoo-ey or something?" prompted Katie.

"Zoe," said Randy. "Rhymes with Bowie. Like David Bowie. I love that name. It's so cool. If I ever have a daughter, I'm going to keep my last name and call her Zoe."

"Zoo-ey Zak!" Katie exclaimed. "Are you kidding?"

"ZOH-ee," Randy corrected again. "Why not? It's different. Zoe Zak. Cool!" She smiled to herself. "So what's the story, Sabs?"

Just then the waitress came to take our order. I was so anxious to tell them about Zoe that I wanted to tell the waitress to come back in fifteen minutes. But I knew everyone was hungry. Katie ordered a large pizza with extra mushrooms and peppers, we each gave our drink order, and then I continued talking.

"Well," I began, when the waitress finally left. "Zoe's dad owns a few art galleries, right? He's decided to open a few in the U.S. The first one will be in Minneapolis. So that's where they're moving!"

"Neat," Allison said as the waitress brought our sodas.

"But that's not the best part," I continued, taking a sip of diet cola. "Zoe's parents have to stay in Paris to finish up some business, so she's going to live with us for a couple of weeks!" I announced. "Isn't that awesome!"

"You mean she'll be going to school with us and everything?" asked Katie.

"Yeah! Since she's twelve, too, she'll even be in our classes. I think it's so cool: I can just see it now"— I paused dramatically, then raised my hand in a sweeping gesture like I was reading a headline — "'Sabrina Wells and Her International Cousin Take Bradley Junior High School by Storm!'" I sighed. "It'll be the biggest thing that's happened all year!"

"She really sounds great," said Allison. "It must be interesting to have lived all over the world."

"Yeah," I agreed. "I'm sure she's really chic and sophisticated."

"Well, I hope she likes it here in Acorn Falls," said Katie. "But I guess if Randy likes it, even someone as international as Zoe will."

Randy and her mom moved to Acorn Falls at the beginning of the school year. It took her a while to get used to it, but now she says she likes it almost as much as New York. Actually, Acorn Falls is a terrific place to live, and it's got lots of great people and stores.

One of my favorite stores is Dare, which is exactly where I dragged my friends after lunch. Dare has the chicest, most sophisticated clothes and accessories. I stopped in there first because

I wanted to get some kind of welcome gift for Zoe. First I was going to get her an incredible green-and-white-striped miniskirt, but my friends talked me out of it.

"You don't even know how tall she is, or anything, do you?" Katie asked.

"Yeah," said Randy. "She could be petite like you, or a beanpole like Allison here." Randy is the only one who can get away with saying things like that to Allison. They're such good friends that Allison doesn't mind at all.

"Or she could wear nothing but black like our spiky friend," said Allison, smiling at Randy.

"Touché," Randy responded.

Finally we went to the accessory counter and found the perfect thing: a super-superlong strand of faux (that means fake) pearls! It was so long, you could wrap it around your neck six times, or wear it in one really long loop. I was sure that Zoe would consider it the height of fashion. It was soooo funky! I really loved it because you could wear it with fancy clothes or with hanging-out clothes like sweaters and leggings. I was pretty pleased with my choice. I couldn't wait to see Zoe's face when I gave it to her.

After our shopping trip we all went over to Katie's to listen to some new CDs she'd bought. This was the perfect opportunity for me to start really paying attention to how the other half lives — the rich, I mean. I've been to Katie's house lots of times since she moved, but now I wanted to look at her new lifestyle from a different angle. I'd even bought a little memo book at the drugstore so I could take notes. I thought it would help Zoe feel more at home if our life looked a little more like hers. She spoke French and Italian, and went to a famous international school in Paris, so I was sure she was used to a certain level of sophistication.

The first thing I noticed was how Katie's housekeeper answered the door. She was so friendly and polite. I thought it would be really awesome if we could hire a maid or something, just for a couple of weeks. But I couldn't see my dad going for it. I could just hear him saying it was an "unnecessary luxury." So I put a question mark next to the word *maid*.

The next thing I noticed was that Katie's mom dressed a lot different than she used to at their old house. I guessed that was because she wasn't working so hard anymore. She now had a staff to cook dinner and do all the cleaning and stuff for her, so I figured she had more time to dress up.

Everything in their house seemed to be in place. Our house always looks like a bomb had hit it. Not that it's dirty or anything like that. But Katie's house is so neat, it almost looks like a museum. I didn't know how I was going to pull that one off, with my crazy brothers zooming in and out all the time.

But the thing that impressed me the most was Katie's stepfather, Mr. Beauvais. He just has this certain way of walking and talking. It's like he's in charge all the time. There is just something about him that makes you sit up and take notice. Maybe it's the way he dresses. My dad owns a hardware store, so I hardly ever see him in a suit and tie. But Mr. Beauvais always looks like he's going to an important meeting or something. I was sure Zoe would be the same way. After all, she was a beautiful model, and she had lived all around the world. I didn't know how the Wells family was going to keep up!

By the time I left Katie's, I had four pages of

notes and I was exhausted. Zoe would be arriving in a week! I just hoped it was enough time to redo my family!

Chapter Two

I spent most of Sunday morning going over my notes and trying to think up little changes I could make around our house. I really wanted to learn more about Zoe and her family. My mom had saved a whole stack of postcards from Zoe's parents, Aunt Megan and Uncle Joel. But they didn't tell me too much about Zoe. My mom didn't even have a picture of her!

It was great to look at all the exotic places they had lived, like Japan, England, Italy, and France. But I still couldn't figure out how to make a little town like Acorn Falls, Minnesota, seem exciting to Zoe.

Finally I came upon a postcard from Paris that had a cute picture of a French café. That gave me a great idea. Food! A change of menu could certainly make the Wells family seem more sophisticated.

I ran down to the kitchen and started poring

over a bunch of my mom's cookbooks. Luckily she had a really big one called *The Best of International Cuisine*. I figured if I could just get my mom to be a little more creative this week, by the time Zoe arrived, it would look like we ate this way all the time!

My mom walked into the kitchen carrying an armload of cans from the basement pantry. She noticed me flipping through the colorful pictures in the cookbook. "I hope this means I'm getting a night off from cooking," she said.

"Could be. Hey, Mom, what are we having for dinner, anyway?" I asked.

"Well, we were going to have hot dogs and sauerkraut," she mumbled as she searched through the pile of cans on the counter. "But I'm afraid we're all out of sauerkraut. What about hot dogs and beans?" Mom smiled, triumphantly holding up two cans of baked beans.

Oh, great, I thought to myself. Now, that's really going to impress an international traveler like Zoe. Hot dogs and beans. How exotic can you get?

"Sabrina, what's the matter?" Mom asked, catching the disappointed look on my face. "You love hot dogs and beans."

"Uh, yeah, Mom," I stammered. "Usually. But why can't we have something a little exotic once in a while? Like . . ."

I stalled, frantically searching for an interesting picture page.

"Like . . . ?" my mom prompted, resting her hands on her hips. I noticed she was wearing her black stirrup pants and brown sweater again. My mom has plenty of clothes, but whenever she's doing housework on the weekends, the first thing she does is change into her black stirrup pants and brown sweater. Not that it's so terrible, but I just couldn't picture Zoe's mom or Katie's mom bringing up cans from the basement dressed like that. I couldn't help wondering what Zoe was going to think of our family.

"Well," my mom asked, interrupting my thoughts. "What kind of exotic meal did you have in mind?"

"Just something different. Like osso buco or steak tartare!" I blurted out. I held up the cookbook to show her the pictures.

"Osso buco or steak tartare," she slowly repeated. "Why, Sabrina, I never realized you were so fond of veal shanks or raw hamburger meat."

"V-v-veal shanks?" I gulped.

". . . and raw hamburger meat," Mom repeated. "Now, Sabs, would you mind telling me what this is all about?" She looked at me sympathetically.

"Well," I began, "I just thought it would be nice if we started eating a little fancier around here, especially since —"

"Especially since Zoe is coming to town?" she questioned, completing my thought.

It did sound pretty bad when she said it that way. But I wasn't ready to give up yet. "But, Mom," I argued, determined to be reasonable, "she has been around the world. How do you think it's going to look if we start serving her common stuff like franks and beans? I mean, I bet she's never eaten a hot dog in her whole life!"

"Then she's missed out on one of the greatest foods in the world," my dad cut in. He had just walked into the kitchen, holding a pipe in one hand and his favorite dress shirt in the other. "Now, Sabrina," he said in a very calm tone of voice, "I found both of these laid out on my bed. I didn't put them there. Your mother didn't put them there. And I'm quite sure your brothers didn't put them there. So that leaves either you or the dog," he concluded. "Where is Cinnamon, anyway?"

My stomach suddenly lurched to my feet. I had laid those things out on his bed this morning. I was just trying to leave a couple of little hints around the house. I guess that wasn't the best idea I've ever had. I cast my eyes back to the picture of osso buco. Now that I knew I was looking at veal bones, it totally grossed me out. I hate veal and I really don't think people should eat baby cows, anyway.

Dad waved the pipe under my nose to get my attention. "Were you trying to tell me something, Sabrina?" he asked.

"Well," I said without looking at him, "I thought it might be nice if we started dressing for dinner."

"And why should I start smoking a pipe and dressing for dinner?" Dad questioned. He placed the pipe in his mouth and stared at me. It wasn't a very good pipe. Actually, it was left over from one of Sam's school plays. I thought it would make a good impression on Zoe.

"Well, you don't have to really smoke it," I assured him. Which was something I absolutely had to do, since my mom and dad are totally against smoking.

"So should I just walk around with the pipe in my mouth like this?" he asked, biting down hard on it. "Or would you prefer a more Sherlock Holmes type of look?" he asked and then hunched over and comically inspected the cans on the counter. His imitation was so poor, I couldn't help laughing.

"I think she was expecting more of the elegant English gentleman type," my mom piped in.

"Oh! Is this what you had in mind?" My dad stood erect and puffed out his chest.

I hated to admit it, but that was exactly what I had in mind. Now he kind of reminded me of Katie's stepdad. But he didn't look quite the same, since he was wearing a flannel shirt and blue jeans. For once in my life I didn't know what to say.

My dad laid the pipe down on the counter. "So, Sabrina, what's the story?" he asked.

"Well," I began again, "I just thought it would be nice if we were just a little more formal around here —"

"Especially since Zoe is coming to town," my

mom repeated.

I just looked at both of them and took a deep breath. They knew exactly what I was up to. Somehow they always do.

"Sabrina, I understand how you feel," said my mom. "But you have to realize that Zoe is going to have to accept our family just the way it is."

"And don't forget that Aunt Megan is my sister," my dad added. "She wasn't always the rich jet-setter she is today."

I gave him a puzzled look. Now *what* was he getting at?

"Actually, we were raised in a house just like this. And it was only a few miles from here," my dad continued. I kind of knew what he was trying to say. But I still couldn't figure out what that had to do with Zoe. Aunt Megan and Uncle Joel were rich and famous. So what if Aunt Megan used to live in Acorn Falls? I just couldn't see what that had to do with Zoe. I just knew she was going to expect more!

"I guess you're right," I said, not meaning a word of it. It was pretty clear that I wasn't going to get anywhere with my parents. I was really feeling frustrated, so I decided to put my household changes on hold for a while and do something else. Zoe was coming in less than a week, and I still had so much to do before she got here! Such as learning two new languages!

You see, the previous night I had had the craziest dream. Actually, it wasn't really a dream. It was more like a nightmare. I dreamed that Zoe arrived, but I couldn't talk to her because she didn't speak one word of English! My mom said that she was fluent in French and Italian, but in my dream she spoke Japanese, Russian, Swedish, German — everything but English and Spanish, which is what I am taking in school.

When I woke up, I was really glad it was only a dream. But I really believe that dreams mean something. And this one was obviously trying to send me a message! I realized that instead of trying to improve my family, I should be learning a little French and Italian before Zoe arrived. That would make her feel right at home.

Since I couldn't change my family, I decided to at least change myself. I spent the rest of Sunday looking at a French dictionary and making lists of words that might come in handy.

All that work really put me in a French mood, so when I was dressing for school on Monday morning, I decided to dress the part.

I wore my navy-and-white-striped polo shirt, a short red miniskirt, black stockings, and a red beret I had gotten for Christmas last year. Then I tied a little white scarf around my neck and put on my big gold hoop earrings. Now I really felt like I had just flown in from Paris.

I got to school late, as usual. Katie was already at the locker we shared. She was talking to Allison. *"Bonjour!"* I called.

Katie scrutinized my ensemble as I tried to find my books in my half of the locker. Katie's always neat, and her half is perfect. I just kind of throw stuff in and hope the door closes.

"Hi," said Katie. "Why are you speaking French?"

"And why are you all dressed up?" asked Allison.

I told Katie and Allison all about my foreign-language idea.

"Forget it, Sabs! There's no way you can learn French *and* Italian in four days," Al assured me.

"It's just not enough time," Katie agreed. "Although you do look awfully cute."

"*C'est magnifique? Non?*" I asked in a thick French accent, striking a glamorous pose against the wall. *C'est magnifique* was one of the phrases from my lists. But I hadn't gotten it from the dictionary. I'd heard it on a French-roast coffee commercial.

"It's very nice," said Allison.

"But it's a little late for Halloween, isn't it, Sabrina?" Stacy Hansen's horrible voice broke into our conversation. She was walking down the hallway with her stupid little clones, Eva Malone, B. Z. Latimer, and Laurel Spencer. Stacy's the most stuck-up girl in the whole seventh grade. Her father's the principal, so she acts like she owns the whole school.

"Well, if it's too late for Halloween, Stacy, then what are you dressed for?" Randy asked. She came breezing by just in the nick of time. Randy's the greatest with a comeback line. Somehow I can never think of anything to say to Stacy when she says things like that. I just stand there and feel my face turn red.

"I'm dressed for class and elegance . . . as always," Stacy said in a prissy tone of voice. "But what would you know about class and elegance, Pineapple Head?"

I guess she was referring to the neon stripes of yellow Randy had streaked through her hair today. It looked really awesome.

I wasn't sure if I should go for it, but something told me that this was the perfect moment to bring up my cousin.

"Well, maybe we could all use a couple of pointers from Zoe," I coolly mentioned to Randy as I bent down to get my math book from my bag.

"Yeah, if anybody knows about class and elegance, it would definitely be Zoe," Katie chimed in, following my lead.

B.Z. was caught. "What's a Zoe?" she asked.

"Who cares?" Stacy quickly cut in.

"I do," said B.Z.

Stacy glared at B.Z. You could tell she just wanted to kill her for showing any interest in anything we had to say.

"Zoe Frances is my cousin from Europe," I said in a very calm tone.

"Actually, she's your international cousin," Allison corrected. "When you've lived all over the world, that's what they call you. International. Sort of like a jet-setter."

"So what's the big deal?" snapped Eva "Jaws"

Malone.

"Nothing." I shrugged, looking Stacy in the eye. "Except that she's coming to live with my family for a while." My friends and I started walking down the hall.

"Then I guess she's going to put her modeling career on hold for a while, huh?" Randy asked loud enough for the whole school to hear. I gave Randy a secret wink. We didn't even have to look back to know that Stacy and her creepy friends were just dying to know more. We just kept walking and talking like they didn't exist. But I could feel them following close behind, just hanging on every word.

"So she must be really gorgeous. Right, Sabs?" Katie asked.

"Glamorous and smart, too," I answered.

"You have to be, if you're going to an exclusive international school in Paris," Allison added, even louder than Randy. The four of us were just dying to crack up. But we knew if we started laughing, it would ruin the whole effect. It's weird how we all think alike sometimes.

We spent the rest of the week driving Stacy absolutely crazy. She knocked herself out pretending not to pay attention. But somehow everywhere we went, one of Stacy's spies seemed to be right around the corner.

Every day that week I wore an outfit with an international flair. Nothing big, just a little reminder.

Tuesday I wore a bright red blouse over my black leggings, a thick black belt, and my black boots. That was for Russia.

Wednesday I tried my best to look sort of Japanese by wearing one of my mom's colorful kimonos over a black turtleneck.

On Thursday I dressed Dutch by wearing a yellow blouse that had a tulip pattern on it. Unfortunately, I didn't have anything that looked like wooden shoes.

And Friday I went Italian. I wore my printed peasant skirt with my white peasant blouse, my gold earrings, and a red-and-green-printed scarf tied around my head. Dressing up is fun, and I figured it would be good practice for my acting career, too! What if I ever had to play a French lady or a Japanese princess?

I was so excited, all I could talk about was Zoe, Zoe, Zoe! By Friday afternoon it seemed like everybody in the seventh grade knew about my cousin Zoe. I was a little afraid I had gotten carried away — I do that sometimes — but I wasn't too worried about it. I just couldn't wait for her to get here. I didn't think that Saturday would ever come. That's when my dad was picking her up at the airport.

On Saturday morning I was all set to go to the airport with my dad, but my mom asked me to stay home and help her with chores around the house. At first I was really bummed out, but then my mom told me how long Zoe and my dad would be with Customs, so I decided staying home was better. Customs is where they check your luggage, passport, and what country you were born in so you can get into this country.

After my dad left, I made every excuse to walk by the living room window to see if they had arrived.

"Sabrina, standing by the window isn't going to make her get here any faster, or help get your chores done," my mom reminded me as I peeked through the curtain for what must've been the millionth time. "Go find something else to do," she suggested.

I finished all my work in record time. Then, rather than stand in front of the window and get scolded, I tried watching one of my favorite videos. But I was so excited, I couldn't concentrate on anything. I just kept looking at the clock.

Finally I heard my dad's car pulling into the driveway. I checked myself in the mirror. I had an all-American outfit on. You know: blue jeans, cowboy boots, and even a flannel shirt. I couldn't wait to tell Zoe that I was wearing it in honor of her arrival. Pleased with the way I looked, I ran to get the door, with Sam and Mark following close behind me. Another brother, Luke, was out. And Matthew — he's the oldest — is away at college. I was just glad they weren't all in the house at the same time. It can get a little nuts at times, and I didn't want Zoe to get too overwhelmed.

Taking a deep breath, I opened the door as graciously as I could.

"Stop acting like she's the queen of England," Sam said. "She's just our cousin."

"We do have to be polite, Sam. She is our guest," said my mom, coming into the room.

Ignoring Sam, I braced myself for my first glimpse of Zoe. I had pictured this moment in my mind about a thousand times. I knew she was going to be tall and beautiful, with long flowing hair, just like the models in *Young Chic*, my favorite magazine.

I watched my dad get out of the car. He walked over to the passenger side and opened the door.

"Gee, even he's treating her like royalty," Mark commented to Sam as they bowed to each other and comically knocked their heads together.

"Cut it out, you guys. She's coming out," I said in a hushed whisper. I took another deep breath as a heavy young girl stepped out of the car. "Who's that?" I asked my mom without turning around. "I didn't know someone else was coming with her."

"That's Zoe," said my mom. "Who else would it be?"

Panicking, I watched as the two figures approached the house. There had to be some mistake. This girl just couldn't be Zoe. She was only a couple of inches taller than me. And her hair was shoulder-length, auburn and wavy. Just like mine. She didn't look tall and glamorous at all. As a matter of fact, she looked kind of chunky. I waited, hoping it was just the shadows playing tricks on my eyes. But as she got closer, I couldn't deny it any longer. My cousin Zoe wasn't tall and glamorous at all! She wasn't what I expected. What was I going to do now?

Chapter Three

Zoe and my father were approaching the house. I had to think of something fast. But I just stood there, staring. My mouth was so dry, I couldn't even speak. I felt like I was in the Twilight Zone. My mind was going a million miles a minute. This was all wrong. There had to be some mistake.

Zoe came into the house and spotted me at once. "Hi! You must be Sabrina," she said, giving me a big hug. "I just couldn't wait to meet you."

I knew I was supposed to hug her back or something, but my body was frozen in place. This wasn't the girl I'd expected. She had to weigh at least forty pounds more than me!

My mom cut in. "Welcome to our home, Zoe. It's wonderful having you here." My mom gave her a big hug.

"Yes. Welcome." I knew I sounded like a robot

from outer space. But I couldn't help myself.

"And you must be Sam," Zoe said, walking over to him. "I can't believe how much you and Sabrina look alike," she squealed, holding her arms out.

"Give your cousin a hug, Sam," my mom urged.

As Sam hesitantly stepped toward her, Zoe threw her arms around him and gave him a giant bear hug.

"Hi, Zoe," said my other brother. "I'm Mark." He held out his hand, trying to get away with a handshake. But Zoe pulled him over and hugged him the same way. I couldn't believe how friendly she was. I figured it had to be some foreign custom or something.

"My goodness! There are just so many of you, I don't know how I'm ever going to keep track," Zoe sighed. She took a step back to take us all in.

"And there's more where that came from," my dad assured her. "You'll meet Luke tonight, and someday you'll meet Matthew, who's away at college," he added, picking up her luggage. "But let's get you settled. You must be tired from your trip." Dad threw me a look and motioned

Zoe and me upstairs.

I knew I had to try to be friendly, but I was still in shock. "You'll be staying in my room," I said.

"Sabrina has to sleep in the attic," said Sam.

"Sabrina has the whole floor all to herself," my mom cut in, giving Sam a dirty look.

"I guess it pays to be the only girl." Zoe laughed as we followed my dad upstairs to my room.

"You can have that closet over there," I told her, pointing to the wall opposite the doorway. "I cleared it out for you. And you can have this drawer," I said, walking over to my dresser.

"Why, thank you, Sabrina." Zoe smiled, her green eyes twinkling. "That's awfully kind of you."

"Well, have fun, you two," my dad said as he put the last suitcase on the bed. "And don't forget, Zoe, our home is your home. Feel free to come down for a little snack later on. I know it's been a long trip!"

"Oh, that would be lovely, Uncle. I did eat on the plane, but I am a bit hungry." Zoe smiled as my dad left the room.

I'll bet, I thought to myself. She probably

can't go more than twenty minutes without eating something. Immediately I felt rotten about having such mean thoughts. It just wasn't like me. Usually I think the best about everyone. And it wasn't that I didn't like Zoe. But I was confused. *And* I had to admit I was worried about what the kids at school were going to think of her. Especially Stacy. After all, this Zoe had nothing to do with the Zoe I had been talking about all week. Why did she have to be so different?

"Sabrina, I love your room!" Zoe exclaimed.

It really is a terrific room, if I do say so myself. My parents let me decorate it, and it's all covered with posters and costumes and things. And today, in Zoe's honor, it was even neat!

"I can't get over how many things you have hanging on your walls." Zoe was looking at one of my many movie-star posters. "My father would never let me put up all these things."

"Why not?" I questioned.

"He'd say it wasn't proper," she explained.

Proper! Now, this was something I could understand. There was just something about the way Zoe talked that was very "proper." It wasn't that she really had any particular accent.

She just sounded different. Sort of British. But the way she sounded had nothing to do with the way she looked.

Don't get me wrong. She *was* pretty. It was just that she was so *normal*-looking. She wasn't wearing any makeup, not even lip gloss. And her hair just sort of hung there, parted on the side. Like it had no style to it at all. I couldn't believe she was rich. And I couldn't believe she was a model! It just didn't make sense.

I nearly died when she started unpacking. All her clothes were so . . . regular. I could tell they were expensive by the material. But they certainly weren't glamorous. A lot of her clothes were navy blue, brown, and green. And most of them were exactly the same. Like, the A-line skirt she had on wasn't too bad, but she had the same exact skirt in four different colors! And I couldn't believe how many plain V-neck sweaters she had.

Suddenly I couldn't imagine giving her the flashy necklace I had bought her. It just didn't seem to fit in with her plain look. Everything seemed so messed up!

"I bought these especially for my trip to America." Zoe proudly held up a pair of blue jeans. "I can't believe you're allowed to wear jeans to school!" she squealed.

"Yeah, we're allowed to wear anything we want," I assured her. "Even this!" I said, twirling around to show off my outfit.

"You mean, if you're in a play or something — right?" she questioned seriously.

"Well, no. . . ." I stumbled. Suddenly I felt really dumb. I did look like I was ready to go herd cattle or something. Everything was going wrong. This just isn't going to work, I thought to myself as I helped her unpack the rest of her things.

"So what would you like to do?" I asked when we finished unpacking. "I have some great videotapes. Or maybe you'd like to watch some cable television. We have almost every channel."

"Whatever you like," Zoe answered. "But before we do anything, can we have that little snack? I'm famished."

"Sure," I said, trying to sound cheerful. "That's a great idea." But as I was saying it, I felt a lump forming in the pit of my stomach.

Watching my calories and eating healthy are a big part of my self-improvement program. I know that if I'm going to be an actress someday, it's important to take care of myself. I've spent months trying to develop good eating patterns. And not snacking between meals is high on the list. But with Zoe around, I could just see myself going back to my old habits. On the way downstairs I tried to remember some of the hints I had read about in this magazine article called "Thin Forever." Suddenly I got a great idea.

If I could set a good example for Zoe, maybe she would start doing what I was doing and lose weight without even trying. I wasn't sure it would work, but it was certainly worth a try.

"How about some popcorn?" I asked as we reached the kitchen.

"Sounds great," Zoe said.

I placed my hot-air popper on the counter.

"What's that?" she asked.

"This is a hot-air popper," I told her. "I just got it. This way you can make popcorn without any fat. And that's much lower in calories," I added, pouring the kernels into the top. "I'll make a whole bunch. We can eat tons of it!"

"Hey, Sabrina!" Sam called from the living room. "Dylan's new video is on! Come and watch!"

"Dylan Palmer?" Zoe exclaimed. "He's my favorite rock star!"

"Mine, too," I said. We ran into the living room to watch.

"Let's dance!" Zoe suggested as the music started. "I just love this tune!"

I couldn't believe my eyes. Zoe just grabbed Mark by the hand and started dancing. I almost fell over. I would never have the guts to do anything like that if I was so . . . big. But the thing that surprised me most was how well Zoe moved. And she knew all the latest steps. Obviously she danced all the time.

Suddenly my thoughts were interrupted by the smell of fresh popcorn. I ran into the kitchen to discover I had totally forgotten to put a bowl under the popping chute . . . and now there was popcorn flying everywhere! The popcorn had gotten into my mom's flowerpots and canisters, and most of the countertops were covered with it. The kitchen looked like it had been hit by a popcorn blizzard!

"HELP!" I yelled. Sam, Mark, and Zoe came rushing in from the living room. "Get a bowl and catch as much as you can!" I instructed, holding up a plate as a shield.

"Hurry up! We're under attack!" Sam yelled. Mark started making siren sounds.

"Popcorn Alert! Popcorn Alert!" Zoe giggled. She grabbed a pot and put it on her head for a helmet.

"Hey! That's a great idea!" Mark laughed, grabbing a bigger pot and doing the same. Frantically we tried to catch as much as we could with our bowls.

After a moment the last kernel popped and everything calmed down. Then Sam, Mark, and Zoe started throwing popcorn at each other. They were laughing like it was the funniest thing in the world.

"Hey, you guys, stop fooling around. We've got to clean this up before Mom gets home," I warned.

"Then we'll have to eat our way out!" Zoe decided, stuffing a handful of popcorn into her mouth.

"I'm with you!" Sam said and bent his head to the counter and started sucking up popcorn like a vacuum cleaner. "Look, Zoe! No hands!"

"Me too!" Mark chimed in, doing the same.

I couldn't believe the way Mark and Sam were showing off for Zoe. They were all cracking up and having a ball. It was like I wasn't even there.

"We have to clean up! Mom's gonna kill us!" I said, trying not to let my anger show.

"Chill out, Sabs!" Sam flicked a piece of popcorn through the air. "We'll get it all clean!"

"Hardly seems worth it," Zoe said. "This stuff is awful!"

"Yeah, you're right," Mark agreed. "It tastes like Styrofoam. But Sabrina loves it," he added.

"So Sabs can have it!" Sam joked. He threw a handful of popcorn at me. Then he opened the refrigerator and started poking around. "Who's up for chocolate pudding and whipped cream?"

"Mmmm. Sounds delish!" Zoe said, licking her lips. "Count me in."

"Make that three," Mark said. He reached for the dessert dishes. "How about you, Sabs?"

"I think I'll pass," I said. I didn't even want any popcorn. And more important, I realized that I really didn't want to go to school on Monday!

Chapter Four

I went through the rest of the day with a sick feeling in the pit of my stomach. I didn't know how I was going to explain *this* Zoe instead of the Zoe I'd been boasting about all week.

When Zoe started watching a video with Sam and Mark, I went up to my room to think everything through. Sitting down on my bed, I went over the events of the morning. I was so confused. When I'm really confused, the only thing that clears my mind is putting a blanket over my head. I'm not sure why, but it usually works.

So I sat there with this blanket over my head and tried to think. But after about five minutes it got really hot under there and I didn't feel any better. Jumping up, I started to pace around the room because that's what people always do in the movies when they are trying to think.

If I could just get Zoe to spiff herself up a little, maybe her size wouldn't matter so much. I could tell everyone that she was a model for large-size clothing or something. The whole idea made me feel a lot better.

I sat down and started leafing through my latest issue of *Young Chic* magazine. That's when I got a great idea. *Young Chic* always has a make-over article in it. The before and after pictures are incredible. Most of the time I can't believe it's the same girl!

Soon I heard Zoe walking up the attic steps. I hadn't realized so much time had passed. Zoe noticed the magazine open on my lap. "I see you read *Young Chic,* too," she said. "We get *Young Chic* in Europe, you know. I love it."

"I like the make-overs best," I said. I flipped the pages until it was open at this month's make-over.

"Aren't they fab?" Zoe agreed. "I can't get over how much you can do with a little makeup and imagination."

It occurred to me that this was the perfect moment to solve the modeling mystery.

"But you must know all about hair and make-up from your modeling career," I said as casually as I could.

"Oh, that!" Zoe said. She gave a little wave of

her hand. "I'm afraid they don't use too much makeup on nine-month-olds."

"Nine-month-olds?" I asked. Now I was really confused.

"Sure. I was a baby model," Zoe explained. "Actually, my last big job was having my picture on a box of diapers in Italy. I was a really cute, chubby baby, so I did some stuff for a baby catalog, and I had a few TV commercials here and there. But I had to stop when I was about five. That's when chubby wasn't so cute anymore. Not that much has changed since then," she said with a chuckle.

We both got very quiet. This was the first time Zoe or I had mentioned her weight. I still couldn't figure out if it bothered her or not.

Zoe broke the silence. "But, like my dad says, 'Only dogs fall in love with bones.'"

"And weight is something you can always change," I added. I was trying to sound nonchalant.

"If you want to," Zoe said. "But anyway, I just came up because Aunt Linda told me to tell you it's time for supper. I think we're having frankfurters. I can't wait. I've never tried frankfurters!" Zoe dashed out of the room.

I slowly followed her. Well, at least the modeling mystery was solved. But that still wasn't going to help me much on Monday morning.

We went into the dining room. The rest of my family was already there and eating.

"Hey, Gabby Sabby, what's shakin', little sister?" It was my second-oldest brother, Luke. Then he looked right past me and headed straight for Zoe.

"And this has to be Cousin Zoe!" he said, giving her a big kiss on the cheek. Then he gestured to a seat at the head of the table. "I believe you get the seat of honor this evening!"

"Wow! This is so much fun!" Zoe said, reaching for the beans. It wasn't hard to see where all the extra weight came from. Zoe just had bad eating habits. She put so many beans on the plate that she barely had room for a hot dog.

"I think it's great to be in such a big family," she said, smiling. "At our house it's usually just me and the servants."

My mom passed a plate of franks around. "How about you, Sabs?" she asked.

"None for me, thanks. I think I'll have some salad." I reached for the salad bowl. I still hadn't totally given up on influencing Zoe about her weight. Especially after our last conversation.

"Sabs is in training for the Olympics," Luke commented to Zoe. "She wants to win the gold medal for the Most Horrible Eater competition. Right, Sabs?" He winked.

"I just like to eat healthy." I smiled as I started on my salad. But the moment I put it in my mouth, I almost spit it out. It didn't even have any dressing on it! But everyone seemed to be watching me, so I ate the whole thing. I kept trying to look happy as I dug into my plate. Since I'm planning to be an actress, I figured it would be good practice in case I ever did a television commercial for a food I didn't like.

"Sure you don't want some nice hot beans?" Luke teased, running the platter under my nose.

"No, thanks. This is delicious," I lied. I felt like a horse chewing on some hay.

"I'll have some more, thank you." Zoe held up her plate.

I couldn't believe it. It was obvious she just wasn't getting the message. Finally I gave up. I just had to face the fact that there was no way Zoe was going to lose thirty pounds overnight, anyway. I decided it was time for Plan B.

"I've got a great idea," I said after dinner was

over and we were back in my room. "Since you love make-overs and I love make-overs, let's give each other a new look!"

"That sounds like fun! You do me first," Zoe said. "Make me look like a typical American teenager!"

I'm finally getting somewhere, I thought to myself. I just knew this was going to work.

First I asked her to put on her new jeans. We had decided during dinner to go to the movies with Sam and Mark later that evening. I thought that it would never do for Zoe to go out on a Saturday night in her tan sweater and olive-green pants with the elastic waistband.

Next I chose her red V-neck sweater and polished her nails to match. Then I added my navy, white, and gold fringed scarf to give the outfit some life. And it also made her look a little thinner. But her hair was a different story. I thought about talking her into a new modern cut, but I decided it was too soon. After she saw how great she could look, I was hoping she would think of it all by herself.

I brushed her hair away from her face and set it with hot rollers to give it some shape. Then I added a thick gold headband that picked up the gold fringe on the shawl. My red button earrings, a little mascara, and some lip gloss did the rest. Now Zoe looked like she almost could be a model. Actually, she was gorgeous!

"Sabrina! You're a miracle worker!" Zoe squealed as she looked in the mirror. "Not only do I look like an American teenager, but I'm all red, white, and blue." Zoe smiled and gave me a hug. "You're really talented. I don't think there's any way I could do you as well!"

"Don't worry. There's no way you could make me over now," I said, eyeing my alarm clock. "We've got to leave in less than twenty-five minutes, and I'm not even ready yet!"

"Okay," she said. "You get ready, and we'll do it another time. I'll meet you downstairs."

Hurriedly I pulled myself together. I tugged on my new jeans, changed into a white shirt, added my gold belt and my red, white, and blue star earrings. Now that I was feeling better about the way Zoe looked, I thought it would be neat to dress like sisters. I ran downstairs to get her, but I couldn't find her anywhere.

"Where's Zoe?" I asked, peeking into the living room.

"I think she's in the bathroom," Sam said.

He didn't take his eyes from the television. "She said something about washing up."

I didn't want to even think it . . . but suddenly I got that sick feeling in the pit of my stomach again.

Zoe came up behind me and tapped me on the shoulder. "I'm ready," she sang.

I turned around slowly. That sick feeling hadn't been for nothing.

In fifteen minutes she had taken off her earrings, washed her face, removed her nail polish, combed her hair back to the side, and changed back into her green pants and tan sweater. I couldn't believe it.

"That sure was fun! I hope we do it again. I really got a kick out of it," Zoe chattered as she followed Sam and Mark to the door.

"So why did you change?" I asked.

"You mean you expected me to go out looking like that?" Zoe asked. She threw back her head and gave a hearty laugh. "Oh, no, Sabrina! I could never do that!"

"Why not?" I asked. "You looked great."

"But I didn't look like me," Zoe replied, like it was no big deal. "That was just for fun. This is the real me."

But the *real* you isn't what people are expecting, I thought to myself.

I was feeling worse by the second. I felt bad because of the way *I* felt about Zoe. I felt bad because of what everyone would say at school on Monday, and right now I felt bad because I didn't want to run into anybody I knew at the movies. What if we ran into Stacy and her friends? What would I do then?

Now I was sorry I hadn't called Katie, Randy, or Allison this afternoon. There are times when you really need to talk to friends. And this was one of those times. But it was too late to call my friends now — everyone was standing at the door waiting for me. I had a feeling this was going to be the longest two weeks of my life.

Chapter Five

By the time Sunday morning rolled around, I decided I would definitely have to change my attitude about Zoe. Thank goodness my parents wanted to take the whole family to Fun City amusement park. At least I could get my mind off facing everyone at school on Monday. Besides, there was no way I was missing out on Fun City! And the really cool thing was that Randy's father had gotten her tickets to Fun City on that very day, so she, Katie, and Allison were all going to be there, too. Randy's father is a director in New York, and he's always getting free tickets to stuff.

Fun City is one of my favorite places in the whole world. It's this big amusement park that has all these awesome rides and attractions, and I knew it was the perfect way to lift my spirits.

As soon as we got to Fun City, Sam, Zoe, and I went straight to the Ferris wheel. That's where I always meet my friends.

We were all having such a great time just being in Fun City, I couldn't even remember why I was so bugged about Zoe in the first place. She was just so much fun to be around. We decided to take a ride, since Randy and the rest didn't seem to be there yet.

"I hope that when it stops, we get stuck at the very top," Zoe said as she squeezed into a car with me and Sam.

"I love that, too!" I squealed. The ride started. Just being lifted off the ground, with the wind blowing through my hair, was awesome. I felt like I didn't have a care in the world.

"Radical!" Sam shouted, looking down.

"Wow! Everyone looks like a little ant," Zoe gasped as Sam started rocking the car back and forth.

"Cut it out, Sam! You're making me dizzy!" I shrieked. I loved it!

"I'll tell you when to open your eyes," Sam said as the car took its first dip. Sam and I always do stuff like that on rides.

The huge wheel started picking up speed. "NOW!" Sam yelled.

"EEE-e-e-e-e!" I screamed at the top of my

lungs, watching the crowd below zoom by. I looked down at the people waiting on line as we whizzed by. I recognized Randy's spiky black hair in the crowd. At first I wasn't sure, but then I realized that there aren't many people in Acorn Falls who have spiky black hair with hot pink streaks running through it. It had to be Randy!

I waved my hands over my head. "Hey, Randy!" I yelled. Randy looked up and gave me a thumbs-up sign.

"What did you say, Sabs?" Zoe shouted over the roar of the Ferris wheel.

"Randy's here," I told her. All of a sudden I started to get nervous again. Zoe was really great, but she wasn't like I had told people she was. I wasn't worried about my friends' reactions. But what was going to happen when we got to school? I had told everyone about a chic, glamorous Zoe, and they were all going to laugh at me. Maybe I'd get lucky and the Ferris wheel would get stuck with us on top. Not for long. Only for a few weeks. Just as I was thinking that, the Ferris wheel came to a dead stop with us at the very top.

"Fantastic!" Zoe screamed. "Isn't this the

greatest, Sabrina?"

"Yeeehhh! We're at the top!" Sam yelled. He rocked the car and pounded his chest like a red-headed King Kong. I guess he didn't realize that we were in imminent danger of being left up there for weeks. But then the wheel started turning again, and I have to say I was relieved!

Finally we slowed down, and the attendants started letting people off. I jumped out of the car the moment it stopped and the door opened. I just couldn't wait to get to my friends!

"Hi," said Katie. "How are you feeling?" I had talked to her last night, when I was still feeling pretty crummy.

"Much better," I said. "Fun City is the greatest!"

"And how are things going with Zoe?" asked Allison.

"Speaking of Zoe, where is she, anyway?" Randy questioned, looking around.

"Right here." Zoe rushed up to our group. She smiled and put out her hand. "I bet you're Randy." Zoe chuckled as she eyed Randy's hair. "Sabs told me all about you."

"Well, she certainly told us all about you, too," Randy said with a grin.

"I'm Allison," Al cut in. "Glad you finally made it, Zoe."

"Me too." Zoe laughed. "And I guess this must be Katie."

"You're right, I'm the famous Katie Campbell," Katie replied. "How do you like our little town?"

"It seems terrific so far!" exclaimed Zoe. "I'm having a great time here."

Sam jumped into the conversation. "So, where do you guys want to go next?"

"How about going to the arcade to play some video games?" Randy suggested.

"I'll go find Mark, and we'll meet you there," Sam said, heading for the Alpine slide.

"I'll help you look," Zoe offered. She jogged after him.

There was a moment of silence that Katie broke. "She seems really nice," Katie said. Obviously she could tell that something was still bothering me. My friends know me so well!

"Yeah," said Randy. "But what happened to the chic international model?"

"That's her." I sighed. "Turns out she was a baby model. The last job she had was on a box of diapers."

"Must've been pretty big diapers," Randy joked.

I stiffened up at Randy's comment. I knew she was only joking, but it definitely rubbed me the wrong way.

"She's not that bad," I shot back, surprised at my reaction. "So she's a little heavy. What's the big deal?"

"It's not just that," Allison said. "You built her up so much and she's just so . . . regular."

"I know," I said. "I mean, I'm totally freaked out. Zoe's lived all around the world, and she's just —"

"Like us," Katie cut in, finishing my thought. "Is that so terrible? Okay, maybe she's not what we would call supercool, but she seems really nice."

"She is!" I practically shouted, glad that Katie was being so logical about the whole thing. We headed for the arcade.

"And I bet she has some awesome stories to tell about all the countries she's lived in," said Randy.

Suddenly I realized that I hadn't spent any time trying to get to know Zoe. I was so worried about what people were going to think, I never even gave her a chance. Randy was right. And so were Katie and Allison. I had the smartest friends in the whole world!

I knew tomorrow wasn't going to be easy, but with my best friends around to back me up, I just knew everything was going to be okay.

Monday morning arrived at last. I was feeling a lot better about the whole thing. Zoe had to spend most of the morning in the main office filling out papers and getting her class assignments, so we decided to meet at my locker before lunch.

"So what do you think of Bradley Junior High so far?" Katie asked Zoe. Katie was waiting for me to find my notebook in my still-messy half of the locker.

"It certainly is different." Zoe giggled. "But I really like it. I think we're in some of the same classes." She glanced down at her schedule. "I think we have gym together, and I have that dreamy history teacher you told me about."

"You mean Mr. Grey?" Katie asked, shutting the locker door.

"Right," said Zoe. "And Mr. Hansen even gave me a locker!"

I was surprised that she could get one in the

middle of the term. "Where is it?" I asked.

Zoe pointed to the far end of the hallway. "It's over there," she said. "And I already met my locker partner. She was really nice to me."

"Oh, yeah? What's her name?" I asked as the three of us headed for the cafeteria.

"Laurel," said Zoe.

Katie and I stopped dead in our tracks.

"Laurel who?" I hesitantly questioned. Which was really dumb, because Stacy's rich, snotty best friend Laurel Spencer is the only Laurel in our whole class.

Zoe looked concerned. "I'm not sure," she answered. "But she has brown hair, and she dresses really well."

"Did you meet anyone else?" I asked. I just knew that Laurel would have told Stacy all about Zoe by this time.

"Just some kids I met at the movies with Sam and Mark," Zoe answered. "But what's wrong with Laurel? She seemed really friendly."

"Friendly as a shark," Randy quipped as she and Allison joined us on the cafeteria line.

"Hi, guys," I said. I picked up a cherry yogurt and an apple.

"Peas or potatoes?" the cafeteria lady asked,

interrupting our conversation.

"Extra potatoes, please, with plenty of gravy," Zoe answered. The cafeteria lady spooned up a mountain so high, you could ski down it. Katie and I exchanged horrified looks.

"Hey, Zoe! How are ya doin'?" Nick Robbins broke into the line to grab a soda.

"Fine!" said Zoe. She looked quite pleased to see him. "Thanks for asking!" She grabbed an ice cream cookie sandwich from the freezer.

"Catch you later!" Nick said as he headed for Sam's table.

We took our lunches to our usual table.

"How do you know Nick Robbins?" Katie asked Zoe.

Nick is definitely one of the cutest guys in the whole seventh grade. He's got blond hair, blue eyes, and a dimple in his chin that makes him look like a movie star. Stacy acts like he's her boyfriend just because they went out in the sixth grade. But I'm not too sure how Nick feels about that.

Zoe looked amused. "I told you. I met a bunch of Sam's friends at the movies on Saturday. Like I said, everyone's been really nice," she added, happily digging into her mashed potatoes.

"Well, that's all going to change in a minute," Allison whispered as we saw Stacy, Eva, B.Z., and Laurel heading for our table. The moment I'd been dreading for days was finally here. I took a deep breath as Stacy approached us. I was getting nervous all over again.

"Don't tell me they're going to sit with us?" Katie gasped.

"Hi, gang," Stacy said, flipping back her long blond hair. She was wearing this gorgeous purple sweater that must've cost at least $75. And she had this gorgeous purple leather miniskirt to match. I must admit Stacy Hansen has an awesome wardrobe.

I couldn't believe it when she and her clique sat down like we were all best friends or something.

Randy pretended to choke on her pita-bread-and-sprouts sandwich. "Hi, gang?" she repeated.

Stacy ignored Randy's comment. "We just came over to meet Sabrina's cousin," she went on. "You know, Sabrina's gorgeous, smart international cousin who's a model," Stacy said, dramatically pausing on every word. She peered around the cafeteria. "So where is she?" she asked in this really syrupy tone of voice.

"Right here," Zoe said, raising her left hand and waving it.

Stacy widened her eyes and gave Zoe the once-over, like she was really shocked. Then she turned to Eva, B.Z., and Laurel, threw back her head, and cackled like the Wicked Witch of the West.

"This is your cousin, the famous model?" Stacy snickered.

Suddenly I felt my body blush coming on. My face got all hot, and then my neck, and pretty soon I knew I was turning as red as my cherry yogurt.

"She's a little on the chubby side, isn't she, Sabrina?" leered Eva Malone. Her silver braces glistened evilly.

"No, Eva, don't say she's chubby," Stacy corrected. "The word is *fat*." Stacy announced this in a voice loud enough for everyone to hear. Suddenly our side of the cafeteria got very quiet. I just sat there frozen in my seat. I felt so bad for Zoe, I couldn't even look at her. Even Randy was so shocked that she couldn't come up with a snappy line.

"And you are . . . ?" Zoe asked, calmly putting her fork down and looking straight at Stacy. She was acting as friendly as ever — like she didn't know that she was the one Stacy was making fun of.

"Why, I'm Stacy," Stacy replied. She was obviously caught off guard by Zoe's question. "Stacy Hansen."

"Oh! You're the principal's daughter." Zoe smiled as she extended her hand to shake Stacy's. "I met your dad this morning. He's really nice."

"He is," Stacy agreed, limply shaking Zoe's hand. You could tell Stacy was totally confused. It was terrific! I guess a couple of years in a ritzy French international school teaches you how to handle things a little differently. Zoe was acting like Stacy was having a normal conversation with her. It was really weird. I'm always looking for a clever comeback line to hit Stacy with. But Zoe's silence seemed to be driving Stacy absolutely batty!

"These are my friends," Stacy muttered. She obviously didn't know what to say next. The rest of them just sat there looking totally bewildered. "This is B. Z. Latimer, Eva Malone, and you've already met Laurel," Stacy continued.

"Hi, everybody," said Zoe. Then she fixed Stacy with an open-eyed stare. "But, Stacy," she said sweetly, "if you know Laurel, then you already knew I was Sabrina's cousin when you sat down."

Stacy turned as purple as the sweater she was wearing. I have never, ever seen her so embarrassed.

Zoe just waited for an answer.

"Well, yes. Sort of . . ." Stacy stuttered. "Except you're not exactly what we expected."

"Who is?" Zoe said, sounding like a philosopher. "Well, *I* am gorgeous." She laughed, playfully batting her eyelashes. "*I* am smart. And *I* have lived all over the world," she continued. "*What* are you?"

Without meaning to, I burst out laughing. Then Randy, Katie, and Allison all joined in. We just couldn't help ourselves. We weren't really laughing at Zoe's comment. It was just the *way* Zoe had said everything, and of course, the look on Stacy's face! I've never seen her at such a loss for words. She sat there for a minute and then got up and stormed away. Her friends got up, too, grabbed their trays, and followed her to the other end of the cafeteria.

Randy jumped to her feet and gave Zoe a high five. "Way to go, Zoe!" she said.

"You really handled that well," said Allison. She reached over and gave Zoe's shoulder a squeeze.

Katie and I just looked at Zoe in amazement and smiled. Talk about not getting what you expected! My cousin Zoe was turning out to be one incredible surprise after another!

Chapter Six

"Hi, Sabrina!" Zoe caught up with me outside our gym class. She had been walking with a whole group of people. I couldn't believe it. It was only Tuesday afternoon, and it seemed like Zoe had been at Bradley Junior High forever!

"I'm glad we're in the same gym class," Zoe said as we headed for the locker room. "Sometimes the first day of gym can be a little weird."

"Did you get your gym clothes yet?" I asked. I put on my Bradley sweatshirt. I really love our gym outfits. Black and orange are our school colors. So our gym outfits have these neat orange sweatshirts with black writing and matching black sweatpants. They look super!

"Thanks for reminding me!" Zoe exclaimed. "I'm supposed to pick them up from my squad captain. But I don't know who my squad captain is."

"Right here." Stacy rounded the corner, carrying a big brown bag. "Remember, this is only temporary," she said as she handed Zoe the package. "We don't have any Bradley sweats in your size, so we'll have to order them. You'll probably take a special extra-large." She was making sure that everyone heard her. "You can wear this for now," Stacy added. Then she turned on her heel and stalked away.

Zoe peeked into the bag. "Well, let's see what this is all about," she said. Zoe was trying to sound casual, but I could tell she was a little worried. So was I.

"Sabrina Wells, front and center!" Miss Hakim, our gym teacher, called me from the other side of the locker room.

"Oops! I totally forgot." I frantically gathered my things. "I'm supposed to help set up the volleyball net today. I'll meet you in the gym, Zoe," I said, rushing out. I had a sinking feeling that Stacy was up to something rotten, but I had to go!

Most of the girls were on the floor when Zoe finally came out of the locker room. She was wearing this pea-green gym suit that looked like it was about a thousand years old. It was a one-piece romper, with no sleeves and a wide elastic waistband. But the worst part was the shorts. They were these big balloon things that were gathered above the knees with the same thick elastic bands. Not only did it look awful, but it made Zoe look about ten sizes bigger than she really was. Slowly people noticed Zoe, and the gym grew very quiet.

Zoe puffed out the shorts and gave a little curtsy. "It's the latest fashion from Paris," she joked. "Courtesy of the House of Hansen."

Everybody turned and looked at Stacy. The gym was so quiet, you could hear a pin drop. This was just the kind of thing I was afraid of. I was starting to sweat, and we hadn't even begun playing volleyball yet! I knew I should say something to help Zoe out, but I couldn't think of anything. All I could think about was how embarrassed I was. What would everyone think of my exotic cousin now?

Miss Hakim came in and started the game. And Zoe was such a good volleyball player that no one cared what she was wearing. They were all cheering and clapping for her every time she spiked another ball right past Stacy.

By the end of the period, a brand-new

orange-and-black Bradley sweatsuit miraculously showed up in Zoe's size, and Miss Hakim made Stacy give it to Zoe and apologize in front of the whole class. I thought Stacy was going to die. At first I thought it was the greatest thing. But then I started worrying about what other little tricks Stacy had up her sleeve. Zoe had managed to beat Stacy two times in a row, and it wasn't like Stacy Hansen to just give up. I dreaded thinking about what she would try next.

After school that day Zoe and I walked to Fitzie's ice cream parlor. My friends and I meet there pretty much every day after school.

"Stacy's gym-suit stunt was awful," I said. "But you really did okay!"

"It's no big deal," Zoe said. "That kind of stuff happens all the time. You sort of get used to it after a while. This isn't the first time I've been the new kid in school."

"Well, you sure know how to handle it," I said.

"It's easy to handle a problem when it's not your problem," Zoe replied nonchalantly.

I gave her a puzzled look.

"The way I see it," said Zoe, "Stacy's the one

with the problem. She's so insecure about herself, she only feels good when she's cutting
someone else down." Zoe smiled. "Actually, I
feel kind of sorry for her."

"I never thought of it that way," I said slowly. I was thinking carefully about what Zoe had
just said. She certainly had a different approach
to things than I did! But it really made a lot of
sense.

We arrived at Fitzie's and immediately saw
my friends. They were all the way in the back in
our favorite corner booth. Zoe and I fought our
way to the back and squeezed into the booth.

"What took you guys so long?" Katie asked.

"We went the long way," I answered. I
grabbed a menu off another table for Zoe. I
already knew what I wanted. I almost always
get a frozen yogurt shake. It's part of my diet
plan — no ice cream!

"We ordered," Randy said. "We were sure
you would spend at least an hour talking to Dr.
Rossi about the dance contest."

Dr. Rossi is the drama coach at school. He's
really cool. But I was still totally mystified.
"What dance contest?" I asked.

"The one Stacy and her gang cooked up as

part of their history project," Allison answered. "The sign-up sheet's been up since this morning. Stacy's father is letting her have the gym Friday night, and she's running this contest called 'Dances Through the Ages.'"

"Sounds to me like an easy way to get the whole class to do her project for her," Randy noted.

The waitress came by and I ordered a strawberry frozen yogurt.

"I'll have a double scoop of chocolate-chip ice cream," Zoe said.

Katie got back to the dance contest. "Actually, it's a pretty good idea," she said. "Everyone who wants to enter picks a time period, a dance, and a partner and signs up in the music room. Stacy, Eva, B.Z., and Laurel are going to research each dance, write a paragraph about it, and put it all together in a little booklet."

"Then, on the night of the contest, they're going to give the booklets out as programs," Allison added. "Mr. Hansen thought it was such a good way to get the whole class involved, he's even throwing in a couple of prizes."

It wasn't fair! I hadn't even started thinking about my history project, and it was due at the end of the week! As much as I hated to admit it, this dance contest really sounded like a great idea.

"Who's judging it?" I asked.

"Probably a couple of teachers," Allison guessed. She stirred her milk shake. "They didn't post all the details yet. But whoever enters gets extra credit, and there's one prize for Best Dancers and one for Best Costumes. That's all I've heard so far."

"Sounds like a lot of fun to me!" Zoe exclaimed. "I know tons of dances from around the world."

Now I was starting to get excited. I just loved anything that had to do with costumes and performing, even if Stacy Hansen was running it. My mind was going a million miles a minute thinking of ideas.

"That sounds awesome! Are you guys going to enter?" I asked.

"Yeah! Let's all enter," Katie suggested.

"Why not?" Randy agreed. "I'll do anything for extra credit."

"I can't wait to get started," Zoe said. "It'll be so much fun! And Sabrina and I can be dance partners!" Zoe beamed and gave me one of her giant bear hugs.

"That will be amusing," I heard a snide voice say. "What are you going to do? The beer-barrel polka? With Zoe as the barrel?"

It was Stacy. She and her best friend, Eva Malone, were in the booth behind us, and they had heard the whole thing! My face turned bright red, and I unsuccessfully searched for something to say.

Stacy snickered as she and Eva got up and headed toward the door. "Well, I'm just glad *I* don't have to worry about getting a partner," she said.

"Don't let her get to you, Sabs," said Zoe. "We're going to have a great dance."

"Yeah," I agreed without enthusiasm.

"Hey, what's going on?" I heard a familiar voice shout. It was Sam. He and his friends were heading for our table.

"Move over," Sam demanded. He elbowed his way into the booth with Jason McKee and Billy Dixon.

"What's going on?" Sam repeated. "Zoe looks like she just won the lottery!"

Zoe beamed at Sam. "We were talking about the big dance contest," she said.

"Sounds kind of dorky to me," Sam said as he stole a slurp of my shake.

"You can get extra credit for history," Katie noted.

Sam's eyes lit up. History wasn't his favorite subject, and I knew he needed all the points he could get this quarter. "Um, Katie," he said. I could tell he was truly embarrassed. "Would you, um, like to enter the contest with me?"

"Sure," said Katie. "But we'll have to figure out what to do."

Billy Dixon turned to Allison. "Are you going to sign up?" he asked. Billy and Allison sort of went on a couple of dates, and they were good friends, so I wasn't surprised when he asked her.

"Yes, I was planning to," Allison answered. "I was thinking of doing this tribal rain dance my grandfather taught me." Allison's a Chippewa Indian, and I was sure that her presentation would be totally awesome. She could get authentic costumes and everything.

"I'll do it with you. A little extra credit couldn't hurt me, either," Billy said.

"As long as they don't take points off for making it rain in the gym," Sam joked.

"Remember, Mr. Hansen just had a new floor put in."

"I'd really like to do it, but it takes at least three people," Al added. "Do you think that would be okay with the judges?"

"Nobody said how many partners you were allowed to have," Randy reminded her. "How about you, me, and Billy?"

"Sounds good to me," Billy said, smiling. "We can work on it at my house after school tomorrow."

Now I was getting a little annoyed. All my friends were getting partners, and no one seemed to care that I was stuck with Zoe. I mean, I liked Zoe and all, but didn't anyone else want to be my partner? I looked to my friends for help, but they didn't even seem to realize what was happening.

Luckily Sam, Mark, Zoe, and I were supposed to go bowling that night at Lois Lane's. Right then and there I decided not to go. I'd say I had to stay home to study. I wasn't going to make the same mistake twice. This time I would call my friends and talk this out!

Chapter Seven

Sabrina calls Katie.

KATIE: Hey, Sabs. What's up?

SABRINA: What's up! Do you really have to ask?

KATIE: You're bugged about being Zoe's dance partner, right? I thought you didn't look too thrilled.

SABRINA: Of course I'm bugged about being Zoe's dance partner! How would you like it?

KATIE: I really don't see what the problem is.

SABRINA: It's just gonna look so weird. I mean, what's everybody going to think?

KATIE: I think they're going to think it's just fine. Everybody loves Zoe, Sabrina. I'm still not clear about the problem.

SABRINA: Well, for starters, it's going to look like I couldn't get a real partner, so I got stuck with my cousin.

KATIE: Sabrina! I can't believe you're acting this way!

(Sabrina pauses and takes a deep breath.)

SABRINA: I know. I hate it! I don't know what's wrong with me.

KATIE: Neither do I. Ever since Zoe came to town, all you seem to care about is what everybody else thinks.

SABRINA: Easy for you to talk. You have a real dance partner. You're going with Sam! Remember?

KATIE: Would it make you feel any better if Zoe was going with some guy?

SABRINA: Sure it would. But who's going to ask Zoe? I mean, I can understand her being friends with boys, but having one ask her out is a whole different story.

KATIE: You mean, because of her weight?

SABRINA: I didn't say that.

KATIE: But that's what you meant, isn't it?

(Sabrina doesn't answer. Now Katie pauses to take a deep breath.)

KATIE: Sabrina, I think you have some thinking to do. What's really bothering you? Are you upset because Zoe isn't who you expected her to be? Or are you upset because of who she is?

SABRINA: I don't know!

KATIE: Then call Allison. Maybe she can help you figure it out. She's pretty good at this stuff. Call me back if you want to.

SABRINA: Okay. But try to think of something in the meantime. Okay?

KATIE: Okay. Bye.

SABRINA: Bye.

Sabrina calls Allison.

SABRINA: Hi, Allison. It's Sabrina.

ALLISON: Hi, Sabs. What's up?

SABRINA: It's about the dance contest, Al.

ALLISON: You mean about you and Zoe? I got the feeling you weren't too thrilled about being her partner.

SABRINA: I'm not, Al! How would you feel?

ALLISON: Frankly, I really don't see what the problem is.

SABRINA: That's just what Katie said. What's with everyone?

ALLISON: Maybe you're the one who's not seeing something. Tell me, what is the problem? You like Zoe. You guys seem to get along well.

SABRINA: I know. But it's going to look so weird. I'll die of embarrassment!

ALLISON: Because you're dancing with your cousin? Or because Zoe doesn't look like you want her to look?

SABRINA: Well . . . a little of both . . . I guess.

ALLISON: Wow, Sabrina! You're getting to be as bad as Stacy!

SABRINA: What's that supposed to mean?

ALLISON: All you're looking at is what's on the outside. Just like Stacy. I can't believe you're being so shallow. You're not even thinking of what a great person Zoe is. All you seem to care about is what everybody else thinks of you.

SABRINA: That's not true. I do care about Zoe. But she's so heavy. Suppose everyone laughs at her?

ALLISON: You mean, suppose everyone laughs at you. Zoe doesn't seem to think it's a problem.

(Sabrina doesn't say anything.)

ALLISON: You still there?

SABRINA: Yeah. I'm still here. I'm thinking.

ALLISON: Well, I can understand how you feel, but I think you're making a big deal out of nothing. Zoe's fine the way she is, and the two of you are going to make a great team. Who cares what anyone else thinks?

(Sabrina sighs.)

SABRINA: All right, Al. Maybe you're right. I'll have to think about it some more. See you tomorrow.

ALLISON: Sabs . . .

SABRINA: Yeah?

ALLISON: I'm sorry if I hurt your feelings. You're not really like Stacy. But remember what I said. Just forget about what everyone else thinks and have a good time. Okay?

SABRINA: Okay. Bye.

ALLISON: Bye.

As soon as Sabrina hangs up the phone, it rings.

SABRINA: Hello.

RANDY: Hi, Sabs. It's me.

SABRINA: Where are you? It sounds so noisy.

RANDY: I came down to the bowling alley with Spike. Sam, Zoe, and Mark are here. Why aren't you?

SABRINA: I had some studying to do.

RANDY: Man! You have been acting really strange lately, Sabrina.

SABRINA: What's that supposed to mean?

RANDY: Never mind. Anyway, you're missing out on all the action. Why don't you come down?

SABRINA: Why? What's going on?

RANDY: You're never gonna believe it.

SABRINA: What?

RANDY: You wouldn't believe who Zoe's been hanging out with all night.

SABRINA: Who?

RANDY: Guess.

SABRINA: I don't know. Laurel?

RANDY: Nope. It's a boy.

SABRINA: Winslow Barton.

RANDY: Nope. Oh, forget it. You'll never guess in a million years.

SABRINA: Well, who?

RANDY: Nick Robbins.

SABRINA: So? Nick's probably being nice to her because he's Sam's friend.

RANDY: Well, maybe you don't get my drift. I don't mean *just* hangin' out, I mean, like, *seriously* hangin' out.

SABRINA: What?

RANDY: They've been bowling together all night, and he's been buyin' her root beers and everything. I think he really likes her, Sabs.

SABRINA: Nick Robbins likes my cousin Zoe?

RANDY: I'm telling you, it's true. They've been laughing and talking since they got here.

SABRINA: Well, that doesn't really mean anything. Zoe gets along with all Sam's friends.

RANDY: I'm not talking about getting along, Sabrina. He actually asked her to be his partner in the dance contest!

SABRINA: WHAT! Are you sure?

RANDY: Can you believe it? Stacy's gonna

have a fit!

SABRINA: But Zoe's supposed to be my partner! How could she do this to me!

RANDY: I thought you'd be thrilled.

SABRINA: Why would I be thrilled?

RANDY: I thought you didn't want to go
with Zoe.

SABRINA: Who said that?

RANDY: I'm not blind, Sabrina. We all know
you hated the idea. Be happy!
You're off the hook!

SABRINA: But I can't be in the contest without a partner. What am I supposed
to do now?

RANDY: Maybe you can be in Allison's rain
dance with me and Billy.

SABRINA: But that's not the same.

RANDY: Don't worry. Something'll come
up.

SABRINA: In three days?

RANDY: I said, don't worry. Listen, I gotta
go. I don't wanna miss anything.
Maybe he'll buy her a burger or
something. Then we'll know it's
true love.

SABRINA: Very funny.

RANDY: I can't help myself. Hey, don't tell
            Zoe I told you anything. Okay?
SABRINA: I won't.
RANDY: Catch you tomorrow. *Ciao!*
SABRINA: *Ciao.*

Chapter Eight

After I hung up with Randy, I flopped down on my bed and waited for Zoe to come home. I was totally confused. I couldn't stop thinking about what Allison and Katie had said. It was really bugging me. Finally I had to admit that I was kind of jealous of Zoe. But I still couldn't figure out what was bothering me the most. Was I upset because Zoe was getting so much attention? Or because I couldn't like her for who she was on the inside? And on top of all of that, how was I supposed to enter the dance contest without a partner? Everything kept spinning around in my head. I got tired just thinking about it.

"Sabrina, are you sleeping?" I heard Zoe whisper as she tiptoed into the bedroom.

I rubbed my eyes. "Gee, I must've drifted off," I groggily mumbled.

"I guess so," Zoe said with a laugh. "You

didn't even bother to change into your pajamas. Can I put on the light?"

"Sure. What time is it?" I asked.

"It's after nine," Zoe replied. She sat down on the side of her bed.

"Well, you must've had a good time," I said, trying to sound casual.

"The best!" she agreed. "I wish you had come."

I acted as innocent as I knew how. "Why? What happened?" I asked.

"Well . . . you know Nick Robbins?" Zoe began.

"Doesn't everyone?" I asked.

Zoe giggled. "I guess so," she said. "Tell me, Sabrina. Is he really Stacy's boyfriend?"

"She seems to think so," I answered. "But not officially. Why?"

"Well . . . I hope you don't get mad," Zoe said very carefully, "but Nick asked me to be his partner in the dance contest — and I said yes."

"Oh." I grabbed a pillow and put it in my lap. "That's okay."

Zoe was fidgeting a bit. "I didn't think it would bother you too much," she said. "I know you really didn't want to be my partner in the first place."

I could feel my body blush coming on again. "I never said that."

"I know," Zoe said. She paused to look down at her fingernails. "You never said anything."

I took a deep breath. I had the feeling this was going to turn into a very serious conversation.

"Sabrina, why are you so ashamed of me?" Zoe asked, continuing to inspect her fingernails. "Is it just because of my weight?"

I was expecting her to be serious, but I never expected her to be so blunt. I puffed my cheeks out and started blowing air through my mouth. It's this dumb thing I do when I'm really super-nervous.

"No, Zoe. It doesn't have much to do with you at all," I said. "It's like what you said this afternoon about Stacy. You're not the one with the problem. I am."

She didn't say a thing. She just looked, waiting for me to explain.

"You see," I continued, "I spent so much time boasting about you before you came. I told everyone what a chic model you were, and how exotic you were and everything. And then when you got here, I just couldn't accept the fact that you were someone totally different than I expected. I was afraid everyone would think I'd been making things up."

"Is that why you've been so ashamed of me?" Zoe asked.

"You knew?" I said.

"I might be heavy, but I'm not stupid," she said. "Of course I knew. And I knew what you were trying to do with your salad and Styrofoam popcorn, too!" Zoe giggled.

"You did?" I blurted out.

Zoe vigorously nodded her head up and down. "Yes, I did!" she said "Believe me, it's not the first time someone's tried to get me to lose weight. But they usually let me know about it first!" Zoe threw a pillow at me and started laughing.

I couldn't help laughing along with her. "Boy, I wish you had told me this sooner," I said. "It would've been a lot easier to swallow than that awful salad!" I threw a pillow at her. Then the two of us fell over, laughing hysterically.

Finally we calmed down. "I'm really sorry," I said.

Zoe smiled. "Me too."

"For what?" I asked.

"For letting it go on so long," Zoe explained. "I should've mentioned it right away."

"Well, at least it's all out in the open now," I said, smiling. "And I'm really glad that Nick asked you out. You'll be the best dance partner anyone's ever had!"

Zoe reached out and gave me one of her big bear hugs. "Thanks, Sabrina," she said. "You're the greatest!"

"No," I said, "you're the greatest!" And when I hugged her this time, I really meant it.

After that, the two of us stayed up talking for hours. It was just like I'd imagined before I met the real Zoe. We were both exhausted in the morning, but it was nice to go to school on Wednesday feeling like my old self. My friends noticed the difference immediately.

"It's good to have the old Sabrina back," Allison commented as we all walked into homeroom. "I missed her."

"Zoe and I had a great talk last night, but I couldn't have done it without your expert advice," I told them. "Thanks, guys."

During homeroom Mr. Hansen started making announcements on that ancient loudspeaker that makes him sound like he's underwater. I didn't need to be reminded that this was the last day we could sign up for the dance contest. It had been on my mind since I passed the music room this morning.

Al and Randy kept asking me to be in the Indian rain dance with them, but it just didn't seem right to me. I felt that not having a partner was my own fault. If I had just said yes to Zoe and not made a big deal out of the whole thing, she never would've said yes to Nick. But it was too late to do anything about it now. After homeroom I went with Katie, Randy, and Al to the music room so that they could sign up.

"Maybe you could put yourself down as director," Katie said as she put her and Sam's names on the list.

"Don't worry, I'm okay," I said, running my finger down the list. I realized that I could have a great time just by helping everybody else with their costumes and music. "Hey, guys, look at this!" I said. "Stacy's entering her own contest! But she doesn't have a partner listed."

"Hey, Sabrina," said a familiar voice, "you are a real dancing type, and I don't see your name on this list."

It was Arizonna. He suddenly appeared right next to me. Arizonna's from California, and he's really laid back. Not to mention totally cute! And a wild dresser. Like today he was wearing one of his California surfing outfits — even though it was the middle of winter! He had on green combat pants, one of those funky T-shirts that changes color, neon-yellow sneakers, and hot pink sunglasses hanging around his neck. Arizonna is really different, and that's what I like about him! I've kind of had a crush on him since he moved to Acorn Falls. And I have a feeling he sort of likes me, too.

"So, dudette, I don't see your name down anywhere," Arizonna said, cutting in front of me to look. "Don't tell me the famous Sabrina Wells, star of stage, screen, and television, is wimping out on a contest. Like, today's the last day!"

I started getting butterflies in my stomach. And my body blush was coming back in earnest. I couldn't believe he noticed my name wasn't listed! I was so excited that I just stood there like a big red balloon, unable to say anything at all!

Randy came to my rescue. "Sabs doesn't have a partner," she said. Some rescue!

"She did. But she doesn't now," Allison added.

"Well, neither do I," said Arizonna. He took a green felt pen out of his knapsack and pulled off the cap with his teeth. I couldn't believe how cool he looked when he did that.

"So, like, why don't we cut the rug together?" he asked, putting his name on the list. "Like, extra credit's the name of the game, and dancin's one of my best subjects."

Now I felt like my heart was going to leap right out of my body. Me and Arizonna. I couldn't believe how great things were turning out!

I tried to be calm, although I really felt like jumping up and down. "Sure," I said. "That would be totally awesome."

"Totally," he agreed as he wrote my name down on the list next to his. "So when do we start?"

As soon as my head stopped spinning, we made plans to meet at his house after school. Sam, Katie, Zoe, and Nick were all meeting at my house. I thought that three rehearsals in one place would be too much, especially since we only have one cassette player!

After school was out, I went home and changed into my black leggings and a black turtleneck sweater. It wasn't exactly a rehearsal outfit, but it sort of felt like one. Then I put on the black dance shoes I had from when we did *Grease*, pulled my hair back in a ponytail, and headed for Arizonna's.

Arizonna's house is a little strange. His father had it built when they moved here from California. Arizonna moved here with his dad after his parents got divorced. His mom still lives in Los Angeles with his three sisters.

Anyway, Arizonna's house is totally different from anything else in town. It's kind of modern-looking, I guess. It has all these weird angles and windows where you would never expect them. Actually, it's really cool.

Inside, it's decorated in what I guess is a Southwestern theme. Just being in it made you feel like you were out West, because there were loads of cactus plants everywhere.

The walls looked like they were made of sand, and almost every one was painted off-white. There were these huge wall hangings all over the place in really bright blues, oranges, yellows, and greens. I couldn't figure out if they were Indian or Mexican. They kind of looked like a little of both.

"We can hang out in here," Arizonna said, leading me into the living room. "I'll be right back."

There wasn't a lot of furniture in the living room. Just a huge off-white couch with a bunch of big colorful pillows on it, an oversized lounge chair, and the biggest television screen I'd ever seen, with a matching stereo console. It had about a million buttons on it. I'd never seen anything like it! The whole room was so Californian — so L.A. I made mental notes on the decorating, because I know I'll have to move to L.A. when I'm an actress. That's where all the action is.

After scanning the room, I sat down on the edge of the big lounge chair. But the second I did, the large-screen TV came on all by itself! Startled by the sound, I fell back into the chair — which immediately started vibrating up and down. That totally freaked me out! I jumped up and hit one of the low-hanging cactus plants with my head. The spiky plant came crashing down with a thud, and I fell back into the chair again. I tried to pick myself up, but the cushion was so deep, I couldn't get up. And now I had cactus spikes sticking all over me! I must've looked like a little black bug being swallowed up by a giant white pillow. Just as I was struggling to lift myself up, Arizonna came back carrying a book and a stack of tapes. I felt like such a total dork!

"Far out!" he said. "You found my dad's special chair."

I just looked up at him with cactus spikes sticking out of my hair. "I'm sorry," I squeaked.

"No sweat, Sabs. We'll clean it up later." Arizonna extended his hand to help me up. Just holding his hand made my face turn red. I couldn't imagine what it was going to be like dancing with him.

"Awesome chair," I said as we both started picking cactus spikes off me. "But I think I'll stick to the couch," I added, taking a seat. "It's safer."

"I've got tons of music here," said Arizonna. He fed a tape into the console. "My dad collects this stuff. And my sister's really into dance. She works on all the shows at her college."

"That's great!" I exclaimed. "I made a list of what everybody else is doing," I said, pulling the list out of my purse, "but I wasn't sure what we could do for music."

It didn't take us very long to choose a dance, since lots of them were already taken. We decided to do a minuet. We figured it would be the easiest, since I had already learned it in gym class.

I had no idea what we were going to wear, so I decided to do some research at home. I always get the seventeeth and eighteenth centuries mixed up. We decided to work out the dancing today and figure out the costumes tomorrow.

Finally we were ready to rehearse. Even though I knew the dance pretty well, it made me kind of nervous to be doing it with Arizonna. Whenever I did it in gym class, it was always with a girl, and I'm used to taking the lead. So every time the music started, we kept bumping into each other and stepping on each other's toes. We had a lot of laughs rehearsing, but it was pretty obvious that we had our work cut out for us. Before I knew it, it was five-thirty, and I had to go. I mean, I still had to start my homework! Not to mention, do my own history project!

I gathered up my things. "So, we'll figure out the costumes tonight and practice again tomorrow?" I asked.

"I'm with you, Sabrina Wells." Arizonna smiled. My heart just did a backward somersault when he smiled like that. "Same bat time, same bat channel," he said, waving good-bye at the door.

That night Zoe and I sat up and did each other's nails. We talked about Nick and Arizonna and our dance numbers. She and Nick were doing the Charleston.

"What are you going to wear?" I asked. I was waving my hands around, trying to dry my nails. "I haven't figured anything out yet."

"Dr. Rossi said we could borrow stuff from the drama department," Zoe informed me. "I checked it out after school today. But by the time I got there, there was hardly anything left."

"Well, what did you have in mind?" I asked.

"I have the perfect dress," Zoe said. "It's the one fancy thing I brought with me, and it's really straight and flappery. I think that's why I wanted to do the Charleston. I just love that dress," she said as she went to the closet to show it to me. "But I really need something to add to it. Some headband, or beads, or something like they wore in the 1920s."

Isn't life strange? Here was my chance to make up for how dorky I had been acting.

"Zoe! Keep your eyes closed," I ordered. "I've got just the thing." I searched through my drawers until I found what I was looking for and then put the gift-wrapped box in her lap.

"What's this?" Zoe asked when she opened her eyes.

"It was supposed to be your welcoming gift, but . . ." I couldn't figure out how to finish that sentence.

"Better late than never," Zoe reminded me as she tore the box open. Then she gasped. "Oh, Sabrina, thank you!" Zoe took the string of faux pearls I had bought for her at Dare out of the box. "I'm going to put on the whole outfit, right now!" she said. She slipped the dress on over her nightgown and then put on the pearls. "Oh, it's absolutely perfect!" She beamed, looking at herself in the mirror.

"Well," I said, laughing, "I really do think it would look better without the nightgown and fuzzy slippers."

"Thank you so much!" Zoe cried, giving me a hug and a kiss. "You're the best cousin a girl ever had!"

Chapter Nine

Zoe and I got to school extra early on Thursday to look through the costumes in the music room. But Zoe was right: There was hardly anything left. I was starting to feel discouraged when all of a sudden I spied a peach lace dress shoved into a corner.

I held it up in front of me. "Hey, look at this, Zoe," I said. "I'm sure this would fit."

Zoe gave it a thumbs-down. "It's kind of dingy," she said.

"Nothing a little detergent couldn't fix." I grinned. "I'll just wash it and add a bit of ribbon here and there. It'll look terrific, you'll see!"

"You sound like Cinderella getting ready for the ball," Zoe said with a giggle.

"But she's going to look more like the pumpkin," Stacy sneered. She swept into the room with the contestant list in her hand. She was with Eva Malone, who was carrying a tremendous speaker. It figured Stacy was getting her dumb clone Eva to do all the heavy stuff for her.

"I don't remember asking your opinion," I said, trying to act calm like Zoe. But it just wasn't me. "So butt out. Okay?" I added. It totally ruined the effect, but it felt good.

"I'll butt out of your business if you get your piggy little cousin to butt out of mine," Stacy shot back.

Zoe looked Stacy straight in the eye. "And what does that mean?" she asked.

"You know exactly what she means, you . . . you . . . boyfriend stealer!" Eva hissed. She put the speaker down, grabbed the contestant list out of Stacy's hand, and waved it in front of Zoe's face.

"Yeah! What's this supposed to mean?" Stacy demanded. She took the list back from Eva and pointed at Zoe's and Nick's names on the list.

"Nick Robbins is Stacy's boyfriend, and everyone knows it!" Eva said.

"He is not," I shot back. Now I was really losing my cool. I was so mad, I crumpled up the peach dress and threw it on the floor.

"He is too!" Stacy insisted. "And even if he isn't, he's got no business going to the dance contest with *her*!"

"Well, I guess you'll have to talk to Nick about that," Zoe said in an extremely calm tone of voice. "He asked me to the dance contest. I said yes. It's not my problem."

"Well, it's going to be when I get through with you." Stacy turned on her heel and stormed out of the room.

"Yeah!" Eva followed Stacy out the door. "You haven't heard the last of us . . . boyfriend stealer!"

"I can't stand that girl!" I was so mad I was hopping up and down in place. I felt like I wanted to punch someone.

"Calm down," Zoe said. She picked the peach dress up off the floor, shook it out, folded it neatly, and handed it to me. "Forget about it. What can she possibly do?"

I just looked at Zoe and didn't answer. I wasn't sure what she could do. But knowing Stacy Hansen, I was sure she was going to do something.

That night I fixed the dress up. I was right! Once it was cleaned up, it looked terrific. I was still a little worried about my dance. Arizonna and I had practiced only for a short time that afternoon. We both had to work on our own history projects. The dancing was getting better, but it still needed work. We had agreed to meet at my house the next day and work on it a little right before the contest.

Now I had to figure out what to do with my hair. This was such great practice! Someday if I had to play an eighteenth-century lady in a movie, I'd be set! I thought it would look really cool if I could do it up like Marie Antoinette's, so I piled it on top of my head. It looked okay, but it definitely needed a little more height. I asked my mom, and she said she had a wiglet left over from a Halloween costume. I took that and pinned it on top. That still didn't seem quite high enough, so I wrapped some toilet paper into a wad and stuck it under the wiglet. Now the hairstyle was perfect! Except for one small detail: My hair is auburn and the wiglet was dark brown.

Suddenly I had a brilliant idea. I remembered what I had learned in history about how everyone wore powdered wigs in those days. That was the perfect solution! I could just put talcum powder all over it, and my hair would be totally white, just like Marie Antoinette's! I was sure it would look great.

The next day was Friday. Fridays are usually slow, but this one just sped by. Everyone was excited about the dance contest. I was, too, but I was also busy keeping my eye on Stacy. That was pretty hard, since she was running around trying to set up the dance contest. I hoped that maybe she'd be too busy to think about getting back at Zoe. But somehow I doubted it.

Sam had invited everyone over to our house after school. I thought it was a great idea, since the dance was at six o'clock and none of us would really have time for dinner. We all agreed to meet in our basement at three-thirty to have some pizza and get into our costumes and stuff.

Nick Robbins was the first one to arrive. "I brought some extra soda." He handed a six-pack to Zoe. "It's root beer," he said.

"My favorite. Thanks, Nick," Zoe said. Then she gave him this huge grin. I couldn't get over how much they liked each other. No wonder Stacy was jealous.

Right after that, Al's father dropped off Al, Katie, and Randy. And all their stuff.

"Wow, what did you bring?" I asked, watching Al and Randy lug a huge carton down the steps.

"You gotta see this, Sabs," said Randy. I could tell she was really excited.

Allison opened the box and carefully lifted out a huge feathered headpiece. "It's an authentic Chippewa headdress," she explained as she smoothed out the colorful feathers. "It belongs to my grandfather, so we have to be really careful with it."

"Wow! It's awesome!" said Sam. "Who gets to wear that?"

"I do," said Billy as he came down the basement steps. "And the best part is, I don't even have to dance much. I just sort of stand there with my arms crossed like this." Billy struck a pose, and Al and Randy placed the headdress on his head. "Isn't it cool?" he asked.

"Far out," Sam agreed. "Wait till Arizonna sees it."

"By the way, where is Arizonna?" Zoe asked. She was bustling around, setting out stacks of paper plates and napkins.

"Oh, I was supposed to tell Sabrina," said Nick. "Arizonna said he'll be a little late. And if he's not here by five, you're supposed to meet him in the music room before the dance."

"What?" I cried. "We're supposed to practice!"

"He said he was sorry," Nick explained. "But he had something really important to do."

"Oh, nuts!" I said. Now I was getting nervous.

"Don't worry, Sabs," Zoe said. "You probably won't have to go on right away. I'll bet you'll have plenty of time."

"I guess so," I said with a pout. I sure hoped she was right.

The doorbell rang, and Sam ran upstairs. He reappeared a few moments later with two big boxes.

"Pizza's here!" he announced. "Let's eat!"

After we ate our pizza, we cleaned up the table and laid out all our costumes.

"Girls get dressed on this side of the basement, and guys come with me," Sam instructed, heading for my dad's workshop.

"Sabrina, I can't believe how great your dress turned out," Zoe commented as I stepped into my peach minuet dress.

"You look great, too!" I said. And she really

did look amazing. Her dress was long and made of black satin. The color and the cut both made her look much slimmer. Her short auburn hair was held back off her face with a headband, and she had put some mascara on, so her beautiful green eyes stood out. And the pearls were the final touch that made it all work out.

Zoe gave me a big smile and tied a knot in the string of pearls. Now she really looked like a flapper! "Thanks to you," she said.

"Hey, get a load of this!" Sam shouted. He came out of the workshop in his sixties getup. He and Katie had decided to do rock 'n' roll, sixties style, and they had raided my parents' collection of old clothes. Sam was wearing a pair of my dad's bell-bottoms and this wild psychedelic shirt. Katie had found a long dress of my mom's. It had this great purple pattern. She had tied a red shawl around her waist so that the fringes hung down. They were quite a pair.

Then Nick came out of the workshop looking totally awesome. He had his hair slicked back, and he was wearing a dark suit. He looked so handsome, I couldn't believe it.

He offered Zoe his arm. "Ready, partner?"

he asked.

"Ready as I'll ever be." She giggled as they linked elbows.

Next I turned to watch Allison and Randy put the finishing touches on their costumes. Randy was putting on a set of Indian beads. They looked fantastic in their ceremonial outfits. They were both wearing matching suede fringed skirts and vests that had Indian beadwork stitched on. In those outfits, with their straight black hair, they looked like they could be sisters.

"Sabrina, you better get a move on," Allison warned as she finished weaving her second braid. "Everyone's ready but you."

I had gotten so involved with seeing what everyone else was wearing that I had totally forgotten to do my hair! I sat down at the table and adjusted the mirror. Then I started piling my hair on top of my head. I rolled up my wad of toilet paper, tucked it under the wiglet, and pinned it to my head.

"Could you help me, please?" I asked Randy. I draped a large towel over my shoulders and handed her the talcum powder.

"What am I supposed to do?" Randy asked.

She was looking at my red-and-dark-brown hair like she expected it to get up and crawl away.

"Just put the talcum powder on my head," I instructed her.

"Are you sure?" she asked, giving me an odd look. Allison and Katie came over to see what was going on.

"Just sprinkle the powder on my head," I said calmly.

"Sabrina, maybe it would be better if you put it on with a powder puff or something," Al suggested.

"There's no time for that," I reminded her. "Just sprinkle it on gently. It'll be fine."

"Okay," said Randy. "If you say so." Carefully she began sprinkling powder over my hair. The room grew quiet as everyone stopped what they were doing to watch.

"Hey, that really looks great," Billy commented as my hair started turning white.

But the second he said it, Randy squeezed the container a little too hard and the top popped off, dumping the entire contents on my head!

Everybody burst out laughing. But I just stared at my reflection in horror. "Help!" I shrieked. "I look like something out of *Ghostbusters*."

Zoe and my other friends rushed over to help. As usual, Katie was calm. "Just put your hand over your eyes, Sabs," she said, "and we'll brush you off."

I covered my eyes and tilted my head forward as they frantically started brushing me off.

"Hey, this doesn't look too bad at all," Randy commented as she blew the last of the dumped powder away.

"I must look like a total mess!" I cried as I picked up my head and looked in the mirror. But when I saw myself, I broke into a big smile. My hair came out even better than I had imagined. I really did look like Marie Antoinette after all!

Chapter Ten

As soon as we got to school, I peeked into the gym to see who the judges were. I was glad to see that Mr. Hansen wasn't one of them. The judges were my history teacher, Mr. Grey; my band teacher, Mr. Metcalf; Dr. Rossi, the drama teacher; and my English teacher, Ms. Staats. I felt pretty good about that. It seemed like a very fair panel.

We all went to the music room to look for Arizonna. It was buzzing with contestants. It seemed like everyone in the whole school was there. Everyone, that is, except Arizonna! I was really getting worried. Where could he be?

The first thing we had to do was give B. Z. Latimer a cassette with our music on it. Then she handed us each a number and told us to find seats in the back bleachers of the gym.

"Let's go get our seats right now, so all the good ones aren't taken," Katie suggested.

"I've got to stay here and wait for Arizonna," I said, pacing up and down. "Where can he be?"

"What number are you?" Zoe asked.

I looked down at my ticket. "Three," I said.

"Wow, that doesn't give you much time," said Randy.

"You mean this is the order we go on in?" I gasped.

"No sweat, Sabs. We got plenty of time," Arizonna said, breezing down the hallway.

I couldn't believe it! He looked totally, incredibly awesome! No wonder he was late. He was wearing a complete eighteenth-century getup. Full suit, embroidered vest, long tails, the works!

"You look incredible!" I said. "Where did you get that stuff?"

"Well, you know," he said. "Like, I went down to the Acorn Falls Costume Shop and got me some clothes. They're pretty cool, right? I'm sorry I'm late," he added. "But, like, I wanted to surprise you."

"Well, you sure did," I said. "It's terrific!"

"But, like, not nearly as terrific as you! Man, you look fab, Sabs. I really dig your hair," he said, looking up at it in amazement.

"We'll save you two seats," Sam cut in. "Try not to be too long," he said as the whole gang headed for the gym.

We found an empty classroom and started going over our steps. Since we had no music, we had to hum the tune. I couldn't get over how much Arizonna had improved in only one day!

"Have you been practicing with someone else?" I asked.

"Does it show?" he said, turning his head away to sneeze.

"Sure does," I said.

"No way, Sabs," said Arizonna. "I just went over the steps by myself. It's much easier when there's only one of us leading." Arizonna laughed and then sneezed a second time. I noticed that his eyes were beginning to tear.

"Do you have a cold or something?" I asked.

"I didn't when I came in here," Arizonna said, sneezing a third time. He sniffed a bit. "Do you have any perfume on?" he asked.

"No," I assured him.

"Then what smells so nice?" he asked. We stopped dancing as he sneezed three times in a row.

Suddenly I realized what the problem was. "It must be the talcum powder in my hair," I said. Already his eyes were turning red and swollen.

"Talcum powder! Oh, man! I'm allergic to talcum powder!" he exclaimed, sneezing two more times.

"Sabrina! Zoe! Where are you?" I heard a voice call.

"We're in here!" I called back. I stuck my head out into the hallway to see who it was. But as soon as I moved my head, my wiglet tipped over and the wad of toilet tissue came tumbling down.

Zoe, Al, Katie, and Randy came hurrying into the room. "The contest is about to start," Zoe said, frantically trying to repin my hair.

"They're asking the first five couples to line up in the music room right away. You two better get going!" Randy added, ushering us out of the classroom.

I couldn't believe it was already time to start. I began to get a little nervous. But then I looked at Arizonna's red eyes and he looked at my flapping wiglet, and the two of us just cracked up. We couldn't stop laughing. The whole thing was just so ridiculous! "Well, too late to do anything about it now," I said as we dashed for the music room.

"The show must go on," Arizonna agreed in between sneezes.

By the time Mr. Metcalf called our number and we started our dance, I was as cool as a cucumber. I guess I figured there wasn't much else that could go wrong at this point. Either that or my natural stage manner took over.

Luckily, Arizonna was able to control his sneezes by keeping some extra distance between us, and my hair managed to stay in place through the whole dance.

"Wow, you two were great!" Katie said as we returned to the bleachers. "I think Randy, Al, and Billy are coming up next," she added.

Now I was really glad that we were number three. That meant I could enjoy the rest of the contest without being nervous.

Allison's Native American rain dance went absolutely perfectly. You could definitely see all the time and effort that had gone into it. The music was awesome, and nobody missed a beat. I was sure the judges would give them a high score.

Sam and Katie were on near the middle. They were doing rock 'n' roll. They had made a medley of all these pop songs from the sixties. The audience loved it. They went wild as Sam and Katie swung each other around the floor doing the Twist, the Swim, the Frug, and every other rock dance you could think of. Before I knew it, the whole audience was clapping their hands and stomping to the beat. They were really fantastic!

"That was awesome!" I squealed as Katie and Sam returned to the bleachers. "You're gonna win Best Dancers for sure!"

"What a great idea!" Randy said.

"When are you guys up?" Katie asked Zoe.

"We're next to last," Zoe said, adjusting her headband.

"And who's last?" I asked.

Zoe gave me a worried look. "I think it's Stacy," she said.

I couldn't believe it. We were all having so much fun, I had totally forgotten about Stacy. Suddenly it seemed kind of weird that she was going on right after Nick and Zoe. I tried concentrating on the rest of the contest, but now I couldn't get Stacy off my mind.

Finally it was Nick and Zoe's turn. I held my breath as they got into position. When Mr. Grey announced Zoe's name, a couple of kids clapped, and some even whistled! I couldn't believe how popular Zoe had become in only a few days. Now I felt really silly about being ashamed of her when she first arrived. She looked absolutely beautiful in her Roaring Twenties costume, and more confident than I'd ever seen her.

Finally the Charleston music started, and Zoe and Nick began dancing. But right away I noticed that there was something very wrong with the music.

"Don't you think the tempo's a little fast?" Katie whispered.

"Very fast," I agreed. Zoe and Nick quickened their steps, trying to keep up.

"I think it's getting even faster," Allison pointed out. Nick and Zoe were dancing faster and faster. Suddenly it dawned on me. This was Stacy's plan! She had retaped their music at a faster speed, figuring they would get flustered and bomb. No wonder she had saved them for next to last! She needed time to fix the tape!

I knew the audience noticed something was wrong when they started murmuring. Nervously I watched as Zoe and Nick huffed and puffed their way through their number without missing a step.

"I can't believe they're keeping up," exclaimed Katie.

"And they're still smiling!" added Randy. "What showmanship!"

"Boy, can that Zoe dance!" Sam commented, watching in amazement. By the time they were through, the audience was on their feet cheering. I guess they figured it was just a technical difficulty. Little did they know that Stacy Hansen was behind the whole thing. Nick and Zoe had to take three bows before the audience let them go.

Right after Zoe and Nick left the floor, Stacy came out wearing this Cleopatra getup. It was so elaborate, I knew it had to be rented. She had a really angry look on her face, and I was sure she was furious that her plan had backfired. I knew she was counting on Zoe and Nick to totally mess up, and then she'd come on and save the day.

Still, I almost fell over when Mr. Grey

announced, "And now, Stacy Hansen and Winslow Barton will perform 'The Dance of the Nile.'"

"Winslow Barton!" we all shouted at the same time. I couldn't believe it! Stacy was always calling him a wimp. She had to be really desperate for a partner to settle for Winslow Barton! When he came out dressed as her slave, everybody cracked up. To top it all off, he kept his glasses on the whole time!

Stacy's face turned beet red as Winslow played with the audience by flexing his nonexistent muscles. He really seemed to be having a good time, but Stacy was totally humiliated. And her dance was really stupid. It looked like she had made it up, because she was doing more posing than anything else. She probably figured her expensive costume would do the work for her, but it just didn't make it. You could hardly tell where her dance started and ended, because the audience never stopped looking at Winslow. It was more like a comedy act than a dance!

When they were finished, Mr. Metcalf called all the contestants to the center of the gym.

"This is how it's going to work," said Mr.

Metcalf. "The judges have picked three finalists for each category. I'll announce those, and you guys will clap for the one you liked the most."

"For Best Costumes, the finalists are Stacy Hansen and Winslow Barton . . ."

I wasn't too happy that Stacy got picked, but I was happy for Winslow because he really is a nice guy. And I had to admit that their costumes were great.

" . . . Sabrina Wells and Arizonna Blake . . ."

My hands flew to my face in amazement, and I screamed as Zoe and Katie ran over and hugged me.

"I can't believe we got picked," I whispered to Arizonna as we stepped out of line.

"It's that hairdo, Sabs," he said. "I don't think there's another one like it in the world."

" . . . and last but not least, Allison Cloud, Randy Zak, and Billy Dixon."

Then Mr. Metcalf stepped behind each couple and raised his hand over our heads, asking for applause. Now I started getting nervous. It sounded like Stacy and Winslow were getting as much applause as me and Arizonna. But when Mr. Metcalf got to Allison, Randy, and Billy, there was no contest. The crowd went wild. They were definitely the winners, and I was really excited and proud of them. The teachers handed them a big bouquet of white carnations.

Then Mr. Grey took the microphone from Mr. Metcalf and called the finalists for Best Dancers.

"Katie Campbell and Sam Wells . . ." he shouted.

". . . Laurel Spencer and Jason McKee . . ." he continued. Laurel and Jason had done the "Great American Musical."

". . . and last but not least, the fastest feet in Minnesota . . . Zoe Frances and Nick Robbins!"

Before Mr. Grey even had a chance to raise his hand over their heads, the whole gym stood up and cheered. He tried to calm them down, but everyone kept whistling and clapping. Finally he gave up and just handed Zoe a bouquet of red roses.

Zoe and I just looked at each other and burst out laughing. She wasn't what I had expected, but she was really something special . . . inside and out.

Don't miss
GIRL TALK #25
HORSE FEVER

"Hey — wait a minute, guys!" Sabs said excitedly. She bounced on the seat cushion, holding up a printed sheet of blue paper. "Listen to this! It's from Rolling Hills Stables."

"Boy, it must be an old ad," Katie remarked. "They've been out of business for years."

"They've just reopened, see?" Sabs held up the ad, which was decorated with a drawing of a horse. "And they're offering a discount on lessons. They're really cheap."

"So?" Al asked.

"We could all take riding lessons together." Sabs's eyes were wide with enthusiasm. "We could learn to ride and jump and . . . well, whatever else you do on a horse. You know — like in those commercials where people are always riding along the beach on a beautiful palomino with a long flowing mane, galloping along through the crashing surf. . . ."

"We're in Minnesota," I pointed out. "We

don't have any surf to crash through."

"We have woods and hills," Sabs said. "Plus we have lots of lakes. You could ride through the woods to a beautiful lake." She sighed.

"I don't think I like horses," Al said, shaking her head doubtfully.

"How about you, Katie?" Sabs demanded. "Wouldn't you like to take riding lessons with me?"

Katie shrugged. "I think it could be fun. But I don't have time right now, with hockey practice."

"Excuses, excuses," Sabs said, rolling her eyes. "Okay, Randy, it's up to you. I know horseback riding is kind of a 'country' thing to do, but it would be fun."

"Not interested," I said, looking away.

"But—" Sabs began.

I shook my head, giving her a very definite look. I was really wishing this discussion would end.

TALK BACK!
TELL US WHAT YOU THINK ABOUT
GIRL TALK BOOKS

Name _____

Address _____

City _____ State _____ Zip_____

Birthday _____ Mo._____ Year _____

Telephone Number (____)_____

1) Did you like this GIRL TALK book?

Check one: YES_____ NO_____

2) Would you buy another GIRL TALK book?

Check one: YES_____ NO_____

*If you like GIRL TALK books, please answer questions 3–5;
otherwise, go directly to question 6.*

3) What do you like most about GIRL TALK books?

Check one: Characters_____ Situations_____
Telephone Talk_____Other_____

4) Who is your favorite GIRL TALK character?

Check one: Sabrina_____ Katie_____ Randy_____
Allison_____ Stacy_____ Other (give name) _____

5) Who is your *least* favorite character?

_____

6) Where did you buy this GIRL TALK book?

Check one: Bookstore____Toy store____Discount store____
Grocery store____Supermarket____Other (give name)_____

Please turn over to continue survey.

7) How many GIRL TALK books have you read?
Check one: 0_____ 1 to 2_____ 3 to 4 _____ 5 or more_____

8) In what type of store would you look for GIRL TALK books?
Bookstore_____Toy store_____Discount store_____
Grocery store_____Supermarket_____Other (give name)_____

9) Which type of store you would visit most often if you wanted to buy a GIRL TALK book?
Check *only* one: Bookstore_____Toy store_____
Discount store_____Grocery store_____Supermarket_____
Other (give name)_____

10) How many books do you read in a month?
Check one: 0_____ 1 to 2_____ 3 to 4 _____ 5 or more_____

11) Do you read any of these books?
Check those you have read:
The Baby-sitters Club_____Nancy Drew_____
Pen Pals_____Sweet Valley High_____
Sweet Valley Twins_____Gymnasts_____

12) Where do you shop most often to buy these books?
Check one: Bookstore_____Toy store_____
Discount store_____Grocery store_____Supermarket_____
Other (give name)_____

13) What other kinds of books do you read most often?
_____

14) What would you like to read more about in GIRL TALK?
_____
_____

Send completed form to :
GIRL TALK Survey, Western Publishing Company, Inc.
1220 Mound Avenue, Mail Station #85
Racine, Wisconsin 53404

**LOOK FOR THE AWESOME GIRL TALK BOOKS
IN A STORE NEAR YOU!**

MORE GIRL TALK TITLES TO LOOK FOR

Nonfiction

ASK ALLIE 101 answers to your questions about boys, friends, family, and school!

YOUR PERSONALITY QUIZ Fun, easy quizzes to help you discover the real you!

BOYTALK: HOW TO TALK TO YOUR FAVORITE GUY